Dedication

This book is dedicated to my best friend Craig Jones. While he is no longer with us he was a big part of helping me realize my dreams of writing back when I was a teenager. If it wasn't for his support back then I would never have even thought about putting pen to paper. I know he is looking down at me with a drink in his hand saying "good for you" while singing along to Meatloaf's "Bat out of Hell."

Acknowledgements

First, I would like to thank my Husband and daughter for putting up with my consistent bitching about getting this book finished. I never thought I'd complete it but now that it is done I feel like I've lost a limb

Secondly, I want to thank my dear friend Sue who looked over this several times to make sure that the story flowed, as well as looking at my grammar. It was a long haul but we did it.

Also Rosanna, thank you for acting as my editor. This book would not have happened if it wasn't for the both of you helping me out at the last hurdle.

And lastly I'd like to thank Dylan O'Brien for being the inspiration for Blake. I've been a supporter since he had his own YouTube Video and I don't think the character of Blake would have ever happened if it wasn't for this guy.

As well as being a great actor and political voice, his kindness to those who support him outshines many others. Many people draw fan art to show their appreciation for actors, singers and other types of celebrities. Well I can't draw but I can write so thank you for being my inspiration and muse.

About the author

Louise A Smalldon started off writing young adult fiction before branching out to romance, sci-fi and horror under her pen name Drake Leigh.

She is married with 1 daughter, a dog, a snake and currently resides in South Wales, UK.

As a young child she always dreamed of writing. Even if she never managed a best seller she knew that as long as she bought a smile to someone's face then it was worth it.

All other works by Author.

Under Louise A Smalldon

Blast from the past: a Cadi Adams Novella

The Man in the Mirror: a Cadi Adams Novella

Upcoming Novellas.

The Mystery of Whitaker College: A Cadi Adams Novella

The Search for Excalibur: A Cadi Adams Novella

Upcoming novels under Drake Leigh

ORIGINS: E.C.H.O.S in the arches

Mankind's Expiration: Rising Dead Series

Chapter 1

Standing in the shadow of the tree line, he watched her as she said her final goodbyes to whomever was buried in the cemetery plot. He did not know her. He didn't know that she had just been orphaned at the age of twenty because of a drunk driver who did not stop at a red light and ploughed into her family, killing them instantly. And he really didn't care. He continued to watch as the tears streamed down her face. She was mumbling. Maybe to herself, maybe to the person she just buried. He didn't know. If he had any compassion he might have felt a twinge of empathy. Instead he just picked a few pieces of lint of his dark coloured and very expensive suit. She was laying a bouquet of flowers on the ground and raw emotion and pain showed in her face for the entire world to see. He just smiled to himself.

Cradling hands to her stomach, she doubled over as if in pain and sank to her knees. The ground was cold and damp from the afternoon rain, but she didn't seem to notice as an overwhelming grief tore through her. It was because she was in this vulnerable position that she didn't see him walk up behind her. She certainly didn't see the way he had been watching her from the shadows.

He was a man who was used to being in control, and seeing a woman submerged in so much pain caused a sadistic need in him to swell. He should be the one that brings her to her knees. A true misogynist, he was a man who saw women only as a means to an end. From their soft lips, to the way they cradled him in the night, making him wish he could crawl inside of them and lose himself in controlled passion.

Shifting his footsteps he studied the woman. In his opinion, she wasn't much to look at, but she had a certain air about her that made him want to take control of her. She was not too skinny and not too curvy. She was just right. She was his type. And she was vulnerable.

He had a disdain for skinny women whose bones dug into him as they fucked. He was not a man who made love to a woman. It was all about him and his pleasure. He needed to pound himself into a woman until she cried out in pain before he even thought about slowing down. He would wait until her passion ignited before hurting her again.

The same went for curvy women. He never liked the soft curves of a voluptuous woman. It was a giant turn off to him. He was a man of control and finesse and he knew how to hurt and control a woman. They never seem to see it coming and that made him laugh even more.

Taking a step forward, he placed a soft hand on the blonde's shoulder, causing her to look up at him with tear stained cheeks and cool grey eyes.

**

Startled from my moment of grief I felt a hand being placed on my right shoulder. This caused me to turn around and face the person who dared to touch me while in such a weakened state. There, behind me stood a tall man in his twenties, with dark brown eyes filled with pity and a hooded brow underneath almost midnight black hair.

"Are you all right, miss?" he asked in a deep, gravelly voice that made me think of rocks grating together. His voice was double bass deep. Standing up, I shook the grass and dirt from my skirt before scrubbing at my tear-stained face with my hand.

"I buried my parents today," I explained, somehow needing to explain my vulnerability. I studied his face and I saw compassion and sympathy in his eyes.

"I'm sorry to hear that, miss. I buried my parents a year ago," he said while holding out his hand. "My name is Carl."
Looking at his outstretch hand, my body started to shake and I slowly grasped it as he introduced himself.

"I'm Laura-Jane, but my friends call me LJ," I stammered nervously.

"Let me buy you a drink, LJ," he offered. "We can both share our grief today."

Still holding my hand with his other hand against my back, he led me away from the cemetery. I never even realized he had manoeuvred me to walk with him right out of the cemetery and into my life.

Chapter 2

Nervously I swept my hand down the cream coloured wedding dress while waiting for Uncle Pete to come and walk me down the aisle. He had flown over specifically for the wedding and, as he was the last remaining family I had, he was going to give me away at the ceremony. After two and a half years together, Carl had finally proposed to me. The wedding was now upon us—the months having flown by until almost as if by magic. Soon I would be Mrs Carl Lewis.

Uncle Pete made it abundantly clear when we sat down together to catch up on old times, that he didn't like him. I hadn't seen Uncle Pete in years, but he had always been over protective. We talked about life on the ranch and how my best friend Blake was making out. He was now helping out at our family ranch, the Coyote Lodge, during the school holidays. And it seemed, according to Uncle Pete, Blake had finally found his first love. Blake was now close to 19 or 20 now and I couldn't believe how much he had grown.

Of course, after all the reminiscing and small talk, it was now time for Uncle Pete to get onto the subject of Carl. He really did not like Carl. I didn't understand why he could not see him like I did.

"I'm sorry sweetheart, I know you love him, but I do not trust him one lick. He has this predatory look in his eyes, and it's not of love but one of possession and control. Are you sure you are ready for this? It's not too late to call off the wedding. You can come home with me and be with your family."

I let go of Uncle Pete's hand and stood up to stare out of the window into the dark night.

"I'm sure, Uncle Pete. Carl is a good man. He would never do anything to hurt me."

With fear in his eyes, he hugged me tight.

"If you are sure sweetheart. But remember, if anything happens, you phone me and I'll pay for a plane ticket to bring you home, okay?" Nodding, I kissed him on the cheek before pouring another whiskey on the rocks for the both of us.

**

So now, here I was stood in my wedding dress, with butterflies fluttering around my stomach. I was waiting for Uncle Pete's knock on the door. Trying to keep my mind and hands occupied, I took the mascara off the makeup tray, putting a coat on each eyelash. Uncle Pete finally arrived and walked into the room, ready to stand in for my deceased father.

As we entered the church, I saw my betrothed standing at the front of the altar. I couldn't help but admire how good he looked in his Tuxedo. The lines of the garment strained as they showed off his muscular physique. As he turned to look at me, I could feel the breath leave my body. No matter what Uncle Pete said, I knew in my heart that Carl was good and kind. Smiling, I reached out to take Carl's hand and he squeezed mine in encouragement.

"You look, beautiful Darling," he said with a confident smile as I stood by his side while we waited for the minister to start the ceremony.

I knew I had made the right decision marrying this man and we would spend the rest of our lives together. We would raise beautiful children together and take delight in the exploration of each other's bodies until we were old and grey.

Chapter 3

As I scrubbed the floor clean, my back began to protest, causing me to let out a deep, frustrated sigh. Carl had lost his shit again this morning when I got back from taking Sasha to school. He kept going on about how my job promotion was going to ruin our marriage because we wouldn't be able to spend enough time together. He would bring up silly little things like why I needed new clothes. He said that my old ones were perfectly fine. Well, they weren't fine if I wanted the promotion.

We argued back and forth for a time. Suddenly and violently, he threw his full cup of coffee at me. I was stunned for a moment. Just as fast, before I could react from the shock, he pushed me into the corner of the kitchen, pointing his finger in my face. He called me a selfish bitch and that it was my fault that he reacted that way. Obviously, I must have done something wrong for him to react like that. It was always my fault. Maybe I did not understand enough about his issues at work. He always came home angry because of something his boss had done, or something one of his co-workers' had fucked up. When he came home furious, he immediately went to the liquor cabinet to pour himself a large scotch. However, even though we had argued and fought the make-up sex had always been amazing.

After all the shit this morning, I phoned my friend Claire—her daughter Kara was friends with Sasha—to ask if Sasha could stay with them tonight. I explained that Carl and I needed a date night to reconnect. Thankfully she understood and agreed. Once the floor was cleaned and all the evidence of the fight erased, I headed upstairs to find the sexy lingerie that I had just bought. I was planning to take some naughty pictures of me in the nightie and to send them to Carl. It has been nearly two weeks since we had been intimate and I was missing him fiercely. Lately he had been coming home from work so tired and exhausted that he usually just downed a six-pack before going right to bed. Sex was the last thing on his mind.

Pulling out the red baby doll nightie from the drawer and examining it, I tried to imagine what his face would look like when he saw me in it.

**

Carl sat at his desk, his blood boiling. He couldn't believe that LJ wanted that job promotion—he made enough for them to live comfortably. When they got married she had said that she would be a stay at home mum when they had children. However, that changed not long after Sasha's first birthday. She got offered a job at a temping agency which she took against his wishes. He slammed his fist against the table hard enough for his coffee cup to rattle, then he sat back in his chair. He had to figure out how to punish her for this. She needed to get it through her thick skull that he was the only one who should be working while she stayed at home to look after Sasha.

Of course, he humoured her when she first got the job, thinking she would eventually get bored. However five years on, she was now accepting a promotion which would mean she would have to dress smartly and work longer hours. One good thing though, he thought miserably, maybe she would have to lose weight now that she was in a higher position. He was finding her curvy figure a turn off.

When they first got together she was a stunning size 8, but now she was pushing a size 18 and all the extra flab was starting to make him physically sick. In fact, it had gotten to the point that he would feign being drunk so he could go to bed early to avoid her. He hated women he bedded to be curvy. All that fat on his wife made him want to vomit whenever he undressed her for sex. Nonetheless, he had to keep up the appearance of being the doting husband who didn't care what his wife looked like because he "loved" her. If he could have he would have kicked her out a long time ago and kept Sasha at home with him. But because of his extra-curricular activities—involving prostitutes, escorts and his new receptionist Sara, he knew he needed LJ there to look after Sasha. He would just have to keep up the act until Sasha was old enough to be left on her own for hours, so he could fulfil his own needs elsewhere.

Suddenly his phone beeped with an incoming text message. As he opened the message he could feel bile rising up his throat. LJ had just sent him a picture message in her sexy lingerie with the tag line, "Sorry for being a bitch. Can I make it up to you later?"

Knowing he just couldn't tell her to fuck off because she turned him completely off, he started typing back a message.

"Hmm, baby I'm so hard for you right now. You look amazing in that outfit. You can definitely make it up to me later."

After sending the message he saw his receptionist walking through the corridor towards his office. With a wave of his hand, he signalled her to come into the office before putting his phone on silent and into the desk drawer. If he was going to be forced to have sex with LJ tonight, then he was going to enjoy himself for now with Sara. As she came in the door, he walked up to her and locked the door behind them. After closing the office window blinds, he kissed her with an angry crushing force, pulling her body flush against his.

**

Carl should have been home by now. Claire had picked up Sasha from school so the house was empty and now I was laying in our bed wearing the sexy outfit. I heard the front door open then close downstairs, before Carl's footsteps started walking up the steps. I posed on the bed and rested my hands between my legs, slowly circling the hard nub. Upon entering the bedroom, a smile lit his face before he pulled off his tie. He roughly grabbed my wrists and without a word tied them around the spindles of the headboard. Grabbing hold of my hair he forced my head up so that I was staring directly into his angry eyes.

"I'm gonna fuck you so hard you will be screaming for mercy," he said, making me shrivel inside. It was going to be one of those nights then. Carl had a penchant for enjoying rough sex while personally, I was more vanilla. But as he told me time and time again, I needed to do what he wanted to please him and rough sex was his thing.

Laying my head against the pillow, he started to grab my swollen breast roughly between his fingers, squeezing and digging until the sensation was just this side of pain. Gasping, he used his other hand to rip away the red silky knickers before painfully kneading his fingers into me. It caused my body to react and tighten of its own accord as the pain started to build. Leaning over, he crushed his mouth to mine, bruising my lips against his teeth before he lifted back up to look at me with even more anger in his eyes.

"I'm gonna fuck you hard and fast for being a selfish bitch to me this morning." Untying my hands he turned me until I was on hands and knees. Then he slapped at my backside with the flat of his hand which caused pain to blossom across the cheek. "You've been a bad girl and I'm going to punish you," he said, lining his erection next to my opening before plunging in hard and fast. Because of the pain, tears sprung to my eyes, causing me to bite down on the pillow. This wasn't making love. This was pure fucking with no care for anyone but himself. Still, I let him do what he wanted because this is what happens when I'm a selfish bitch. He punishes me and I just take it.

As he pounded harder and harder into me I could feel the pain between my legs getting worse. I bit down on the pillow to stop the scream of agony which was about to be ripped from my throat. If I did that, then he would find other ways to make me suffer. After what seems like hours his rhythm started to falter and I know he was close to finishing. I breathed a sigh of relief when he finally stopped and pulled himself out of me. He slapped me once more on the behind before leaving the room without a word. When he was gone, I curled up on the bed and cried. This was not the night of sweet lovemaking I had envisioned, but of animalistic fucking. Why did I have to be such a bitch to him?

Chapter 4

"Morning sunshine." Looking up I saw my daughter standing in the door with her book bag in her hand. "Let's get you breakfast and then I'll drop you off at school on my way to work." 12-year-old Sasha looked at me with her big brown eyes before rolling them in my direction.

She pushed her long blonde hair from her face. And said,

"I'll get something at school, Mum. I need to meet Kara before registration." She lifted her bag up to her shoulder, before grabbing my keys from the hook by the door. "When is Daddy coming home?" she asked, perching on the arm of the chair. I gave her a look of disapproval and she immediately slid into the seat of the chair. Carl had been working non-stop for weeks on end. He hadn't spent one night in our bed due to his work for the last fortnight. Both Sasha and I were missing him terribly.

"He says he will be home tonight." Picking up my handbag, I moved her towards the door, "He said he will make sure he comes in to say goodnight to you when he gets back." As Sasha left the room I smiled to myself. I was glad he was finally coming home. The house was so quiet without his quick wit and schoolboy smile. Worry slowly churned in my stomach. I felt that he was distancing himself from our home and bed. In the last twelve years of our marriage, I had put on weight and was now twice the size I was when we first met. However, in the last month or so I had shed a stone in weight. I was now feeling so much better about myself. So much so that I had even bought a new kinky outfit that I would be wearing to bed when he came home. Hopefully he will be blown away by the outfit and we will cement our physical relationship again. Maybe I would start hearing the words I love you again. The last couple of months, he wouldn't even say it on the phone which both annoyed and worried me. Is he falling out of love with me? Or worse yet, had he already? Tonight I would hopefully know the answer.

**

As I left work, the news broke that there had been a ten-car pileup on the motorway. This had caused the main road out of the town to be closed until the police and EMS could clear the scene. That meant that I wouldn't be able get back in time to pick Sasha up from school. Pulling my phone from the purse, I noticed several missed calls from Carl. However, when I returned the call they went unanswered. I pulled up Sasha's number to text her and let her know that I was going to be late. I instructed her to walk to Kara's where I would pick her up.

Shaking my head, I could see that the traffic was turning into gridlock. I brought my car to a stop at the junction and, although it would add another thirty minutes to the drive to the sleepy village of Pentraf Fach that we call home, I chose to take the long way home. I just hoped that not too many other people would also decide to take the treacherous route home. It was bad enough when one car drove on it. Adding a few hundred more cars could be disastrous.

The stretch of country road is full of twists and turns. Sometimes you could see a sudden drop off before once again lush green fields hugged the side of the road. Wild pansies and daisies bobbed in the subtle breeze, their heads jumping to and fro manically as the wind from the passing vehicles disturbed their dance, before finally settling once again into the gentle bobbing. Quite suddenly my phone rang, causing me to jump as it quickly cut off the music floating through my speakers. Glancing at the caller ID, I saw it was Carl so I answered the phone.

"Hi honey. Are you caught in the traffic on the motorway?" I asked him, settling back into the seat.

"I was, but now I'm on that bloody twisty road," Carl said.

Looking up at the mirror I smiled, hoping to see him in my rear view mirror. For as long as I have known Carl, he had avoided this road with a passion. Unlike me, who was a country girl, he was a city boy and was not used to winding roads.

"Me too..." Just as I'm about to carry on my conversation I saw a red car zooming towards me. Quickly, I pulled onto the side of the road before he crashed straight into me, "You stupid fucking idiot!" I yelled out of the window as he screeched past me. He actually had the nerve to give me the finger out of his BMW window. "Learn to fucking drive!" I turned my attention back to my husband. "Be careful Carl, if you are behind me on the road there is an idiot coming your way." Closing the window half-way I lit a cigarette to calm my nerves, "Someone obviously is driving Daddy's car."

"You always say that about young drivers," he said laughing.

Huffing, I was about to say something further when I heard the unmistakable screech of breaking tyres and then crashing metal coming from the tinny speaker off my phone. "Carl?"

Silence...

"Carl!" I screamed into the phone.

I immediately turned the car around and raced up the road to see if I could find the source of the ominous sounds. Shaking I drove around a corner and saw my husband's car, or what was left of it. Now it was nothing short of scrap metal, while the BMW that had passed me was facing my direction. Both cars were crumbled. Pulling in next to them, I could see the driver of the BMW pulling himself out of the wreckage with nothing more than a few cuts and bruises. Meanwhile my husband's car remained eerily quiet. The only sounds that could be heard were of the disturbed crickets and the hissing steam coming from the car's radiator.

Dread settled in my stomach as I pulled to a stop and opened the car door. My phone clutched in my hands like a lifeline, I hoped to find some sign of life from within the depths of the Carl's car, but the silence continued. The only sound I could hear was the beating of my own heart. Crying, I placed my hand on the door. I could see Carl's bloodied arm hanging out of the window. I closed my eyes and took a deep breath before looking into the cabin of the car.

In films, you knew when someone was dead because their eyes, which once held the light of life in them were glazed over. What they don't tell you in the films was that even though death looks silent it isn't. Even though the eyes might be glazed over, the dripping blood echoes and leaves a mark in your soul like a black spot on a soon to be rotten piece of fruit. It festers and petrifies until there was nothing left but despair and utter hopelessness.

Looking at my husband's dark brown eyes glazed over in death, I realized that I would never hear his laugh again, or see the way his eyes would crinkle with slight crow's feet when he laughed at something on the television. Or the way he would continuously moan about his dark hair was getting greyer. I'd never again feel his touch as his hands skimmed over my body while we made love into the early hours of the morning. Then my mind went to Sasha and the fact that she would never see her dad again, never share their first father-daughter dance or have him walk her down the aisle when she finally found Mister Right.

Not knowing how to react I fell to my knees and just stared at the man who had given me thirteen amazing years and a beautiful daughter while his eyes stared lifelessly out of the shattered window at the scenery in front of us.

**

When I finally got home from picking Sasha up we sat in the living room and just stared blankly at the wall. We were both in shock, too emotionally drained to even contemplate a conversation. It had been just the three of us for so long. Both of our parents had been gone for a long time meaning Sasha had never known her grandparents. It was just us against the world now. After the police and coroner had turned up at the crash site I had to pull myself together and somehow tell Sasha that her father was gone. Nothing in the world could have prepared me for the look in her eyes when I finally told her.

Those same brown eyes were now staring hauntingly at the wall, shock plain on her features and in her movements as she took in what she had been told. She cried when I told her, but now she was silent, without a word or sound escaping her lips. Wanting to hug her, I leaned forward to take her in my arms, but pain filled my body as she pushed me away and walked off up to her room. She had not accepted a hug from me for years, so I didn't know why this would be any different. She was Daddy's girl while I was just the woman who had given birth to her. We had never seen eye to eye due to the fact she was Carl's girl, our personalities completely different like chalk and cheese. It still hurt that she would not even come to me for a hug in her time of despair.

Taking a look around the room I realized one thing; no matter what, we couldn't stay here. The memories and emotions were too raw. There was only one place I wanted to be and that was back at the ranch with our last remaining family. I wanted to go to the only other place I called home. How I was going to tell Sasha that we need to leave our home?

Chapter 5

Organizing the funeral was hard. I had no one to help me due to the fact that my only family were thousands of miles away. I made the decision to phone the only other person who I hoped would be able to help me through this dark time. I needed his happy go lucky attitude to get me through these trying times. Making sure the time difference would not be an issue, I dialled the number of my first and only true friend... Blake Dylan.

The floor creaked as I paced the floor, waiting for the call to connect. Hoping to calm my nerves, I took out a cigarette and eased myself into a chair. The summer room was officially my smoking area. As the call connected, I dropped the cigarette in my lap, causing me to burn my leg in the process.

"Howdy," Blake said. His voice rumbled through the telephone line and it caused my heart to tremor ever so slightly. I had to let my heart settle back to its normal rhythm before I was able to speak. "LJ is that you?" he whispered softly. My emotions swelled until I could no longer hold on to my feelings. In between heart breaking sobs, tears cascaded down my cheeks. "LJ, honey, speak to me." Choking back my tears I tried to make a coherent sentence.

"Bl—Blake…" Merely saying his name caused all my emotions to come boiling to the surface. "I need help. I don't know what else to do." Sniffing, I stubbed out the cigarette into the ashtray and just sat back in the chair. I pulled Carl's jumper from off the back of the surrounding seat and hugged it close to my chest. "I don't know how to do this without him."

"I'll speak to Pete and fly over. Ya shouldn't be alone at a time like this."

Even though I would have loved to have him holding my hand, I shook my head, leaning against the edge of the chair.

"No, you can't. Uncle Pete needs you there." As much as I needed help and emotional support, I couldn't take him away from my Uncle.

"Yes, I can, and I won't hear you say otherwise. Pete won't mind. It's taken all of us to stop him hopping on the next flight over to help ya. He wants to bring ya home to us." A smile touched my lips as I remembered how the conversation went with my Uncle a couple of days before.

"LJ, I'm coming to you. I can't let my niece struggle on her own. Your momma would be turning in her grave if I didn't. Ya need to come home," Uncle Pete had said adamantly.

"Actually I wouldn't mind the help. Sasha just hides in her room. She won't even speak to me and barely eats enough for a rabbit to survive on." Truth be told I had been worried about her this last week. She hadn't gone to school because I thought she needed the time to grieve. But then again, she needed to talk to me and tell me what she was feeling. "I'm the only one she has left, and she won't even look at me."

"Look LJ, I'm booking a flight tonight from Austin and I'll message ya to let y'all know what time I'm getting there tomorrow." He wasn't going to take no for an answer. He wished me a good night before hanging up the phone.

A sense of peace and nervousness enveloped me. Blake and I hadn't seen each other for years, yet he would drop everything in a heartbeat to help me. Getting up out of the chair I headed upstairs to attempt to get some sleep. Any rest was welcomed before the nightmares I knew came back to terrorize me again.

**

Screams echoed around my room as I jumped out of my bed. I was shivering due to the lingering effects of the nightmare. All of them in the past week had been a vivid replay of the crash in high definition. This time though, not only had I peered in the car and seen my husband dead at the wheel, but the blood had begun pooling from the door, stretching out towards my feet. Every time I moved back to escape the red puddle, it would creep closer until I had nowhere to run. It would cover my feet and creep up my body until it reached my mouth. I would wake up screaming and shaking in my own bed. I knew sleep was no longer an option so I picked up my phone from the table before quietly walking downstairs. I sat at the mahogany breakfast bar and watched the sun rise. Another day I had to face without Carl.

As the coffee maker started to boil, I opened up the door and lit up my first of many cigarettes of the day. I had to start buying rolling tobacco as I was spending a small fortune on store bought cigarettes. The coffee maker spit out the last of the fresh brew telling me that it was ready. I looked down at my phone and saw a message from Blake.

"Hi Darlin' I'm catching the 8 pm flight from Austin so I should be at Cardiff by 6 pm your time tomorrow. B X."

It took me a moment to realize that I only had about ten hours to tidy up the spare room before driving to Cardiff airport to pick him up. Putting my cigarette out in the ashtray, I poured a large coffee cup and headed upstairs to clear out the spare room. Even though he was coming to help, I was a little excited to see him. It had been such a long time.

**

I swept the last of the dust from the room and was surprised when Sasha walked into the room to ask what I was doing. After explaining all to her, she shockingly began to help me by getting fresh linen out of the Ottoman and making the bed. I finished dusting the room and examined my work. I hadn't been in the spare bedroom for a long time. It was Carl's go to place when he came home late from work and didn't want to disturb me. A sense of ease filled my chest when Sasha started talking to me and asking questions about Blake.

She was suddenly very curious about my long-time family friend. She wanted to know everything there was about Blake. She wanted to know how we first met and why I never really mentioned him to her before. She seemed to be excited to meet my cowboy pen-friend. Sasha had always felt an affinity for horses and always dreamed about moving to Texas when she was older. She wanted to have her own ranch full of horses. Since the age of five, Carl and I had paid for her to have horse riding lessons so that she would be comfortable on a horse when we went on treks across the Brecon Beacons.

"Mama, do you think he will be able to take me horse riding while he is here?" she asked in a quiet husky voice. "I mean he does rodeo, so he may not want to take a kid riding." She looked at me with tears in her eyes. It had always been her Daddy who would take her riding if I had been stuck at work. My heart clenched in grief.

"I'm sure he will. I told him that you were taking riding lessons. He was so happy. In fact, I still have his letter. Would you like to read it?" I reached into my keepsake box where I kept all my letters and pictures from Blake. She nodded her head as I shuffled through the letters before finding the correct one and handed it to her.

"LJ darlin', I'm glad that you are all doing well and my oh my Sasha is a sweet little thang. I love the picture you sent me of the two of you. It is now hanging in my trailer. I'm glad you have started her with riding lessons. Maybe when you come and visit us, we can all go riding together. I know Pete would be glad of your company on the trails as he misses you so much. We will have her bucking broncos before you know it.

I know this letter is short, but I'm about to hit the rodeo again. I'm just glad your Uncle lets me spend time away from the ranch for weeks at a time to do this. However, nothing beats a good old Texas barbeque when I come home. Since your Aunt Clara died your Uncle has completely changed his life. He doesn't drink as much anymore and he is getting really good at cooking a mean ole steak.

I need to go darlin'. Billy-Jo is waiting for me with the truck and my bronco Bertha. She is a mean and wily thing, but she has helped me win a few times now. I hope you like the belt buckle I have included. I won it on my last circuit and wanted you to have it so you had a piece of home with you. I know y'all class yourself as British, but you will always be my American lass and friend. Say howdy to Carl for me and give little Sasha a great big hug from her Uncle Blake. Talk to you soon darlin'. B X."

"Where is the belt buckle mama?" Sasha asked. I rummaged around the box and pulled out a handkerchief. I unwrapped the cloth to reveal the brass buckle with an engraving of a bucking stallion with a rider swirling his hat in the air. I could almost imagine the cowboy saying "yee-haw" as he tried to hold on for the designated eight seconds and more.

After giving it to her, I let her have a few moments to study it before leaving her alone and heading downstairs. I needed to grab my bag before we had to leave for the airport. A few minutes later, Sasha followed me down the stairs. I noticed the belt buckle was now attached to her own belt. I smiled. It went well with the dark jeans and cowboy boots she wore.

"Mama?" she said as I ushered her out of the door.

"Yes, Dove." I answered while checking to make sure the front door was locked.

"Do you think Blake will like me?" she asked sincerely. "And do you think Daddy would be okay with it if Blake took me horse riding?"

Tears started to fill my eyes and I hugged her tightly.

"I know Daddy would be happy if Blake took you riding. And of course Blake will like you too." I opened the passenger door and waited for Sasha to get in the car. "He has seen pictures of you growing up, and he has been waiting for a long to meet you." She smiled and my heart fluttered. I realized that this was the first time in a long time that I've seen her angelic smile.

Chapter 6

Once we arrived at the airport, I could see that there was still a good thirty minutes before Blake's flight was due to land. Sasha and I headed to a little coffee shop in the terminal to get a couple of hot drinks while we waited. I ordered a mocha for myself and hot chocolate for Sasha along with a few tea cakes. The coffee shop had a nice outdoor deck where we could enjoy our coffee and cake in the cool night air.

"What was Blake like growing up, Mama?" Sasha asked as she sipped her hot chocolate.

"Well, Dove, he was only seven when we first met and he was a character even then. He was always hanging around the ranch with your great Uncle. I've never seen a boy get into so many accidents in my life. One day when he was about ten years old, I found him hanging from a tree branch by his belt." I smiled fondly at the memory, "He found a baby bird at the base of the tree. It must have fallen out of the nest. Being a fearless and kind hearted soul, he decided to return it to its nest before his mama got scared." Laughing at this memory, I lit up a cigarette and took a long inhale of smoke before continuing my story. "He managed to climb up the tree and get the baby bird back in its nest, however, on the way back down his foot slipped off a branch and he ended up hanging by his britches. He was probably the luckiest kid on the planet or the most accident prone." Sasha looked up at me with wonder and expectant eyes.

Hanging on to my every word, Sasha asked, "Then what happened, Mama? Was he up there all night?"

Shaking my head, I continued the story.

"No Dove. I was down by the lake enjoying a bit of alone time. You see I'm three years older than Blake—a typical teenager by then. I had enough of this ten-year-old kid running around and needed a bit of quiet time. He was like a little brother to me, but sometimes I needed a break from all his antics. I was there sunning myself in the hot Texas sun trying to get a tan. Anyway, out of nowhere I heard this voice scream for help. I thought maybe a coyote had got onto the ranch property and it was terrorizing the livestock. When I finally got to the tree, I looked up and there was Blake hanging there by the seat of his pants with tears running down his face. It took me a good half an hour to get him down from his predicament. He was so embarrassed that he made me promise not to tell anyone what happened. Of course, Uncle Pete saw the whole thing, but instead of helping he took photographs. Every year on his birthday, Blake gets a photo of him dangling from the tree. He still doesn't know who sends it to him." Sasha started giggling loudly at the images of this poor kid dangling from a tree branch. After a few minutes, we heard the announcement over the PA system that the Austin Texas flight had landed.

"Come on, Dove, we should go and meet Blake at the gate."

**

We waited at the gate for the plane to unload its passengers. I found myself pacing the floor like an expectant parent. It was typical that Blake would probably be letting everyone else disembark first. He was a gentleman like that. We didn't have to wait too long though. I finally saw the top of his Stetson hat over the crowd of people walking toward us. I didn't even realize that I was holding my breath until I let out a long sigh on the exhale. I saw the tall and very familiar figure slowly emerge from the thinning crowd. An angelic beam of light caught his face as he walked down the corridor. I could see his brown eyes twinkling with an inner laughter that he always had since childhood and the dimples on his cheeks gave him his hundred-watt smile. His eagle eye vision spotted me in the crowd and he quickened his pace toward us. Soon I found myself enveloped in a pair of strong arms. Even after a 15-hour flight, just a hint of horses and hay lingered on his clothes and I was immediately transported back to the ranch where I spent my childhood.

"Hi, Darlin', long time no see," he said in his thick Texan accent. "How ya keeping?"

"I'm all right. Just struggling a bit, you know." My voice was muffled in his black leather jacket. I slowly pulled back from his embrace so I could introduce him to Sasha. Noticing the guitar case strapped to his back, I said, "Well, you didn't mention that you played guitar in your letters. How long have you been doing that?" I took a step back and pulled Sasha into me. She had gone really quiet all of a sudden. She was blushing so much that I could feel the heat coming off of her. I couldn't blame her. Blake looked fantastic. H squatted down to look at Sasha.

Tipping his hat at her, he said in a long, slow drawl,

"Well, little lady, aren't ya a beautiful lass. Ya look just like your mama when she was only a touch older than you." He smiled at her before he took her hand in his own and kissed the knuckles lightly. "Sasha, I'm Blake. It's a pleasure to meet ya, little Darlin." With a smile, she nodded her head at him, then hid shyly behind me. "Well I don't know about ya ladies, but I'm so tired. Jet lag is a B--." He looked at Sasha and held back his cussing. "Um, Jet lag is not fun."

"So what is with the guitar?" I swung his backpack over my shoulder as we started to walk out of the airport into the cool Welsh night.

"Well the Rodeo circuit can get a little lonely, so we all get together with our guitars and do a guitar-pull."

"What's a guitar-pull?" Sasha asked.

"Well, little lady, back in the old days of rodeos, the guys and gals would get together with one guitar and entertain each other with songs and stories. The reason it was called a pull was because sometime you had to pull the guitar away to have your turn. Not so much nowadays. Most folk have their own guitars. Hey, if ya are lucky, I'll play y'all a song. Plus if I recall ya have a sweet little voice. Maybe we can do a duet together." He draped his arm over my shoulders and gave me a quick squeeze. "How are ya anyway, Darlin'? How are ya doing?" Wiping away the tears that have started to pool in my eyes I shrugged my shoulders slightly.

"I'm okay, really. Just trying to keep strong for Sasha. I'll breakdown eventually, but not yet. I've got too much to do." He smiled as he pulled us to a stop in the middle in the car park before he placed a calloused hand against my cheek. He wiped away the tears that have escaped my eyes with his thumb.

"I'm here now, Darlin', and I'll help y'all out for as long as ya need." Smiling he kissed me lightly on the forehead. "Now let's mosey on to your house. I can't wait to see this Pentraf Fach that I heard so much about in the daylight." When we get to the car he opened the doors so Sasha and I could enter first, then made his way around the other side. Sitting in the seat, he looked me square in the eye. "After this is over, why don't ya and Sasha come to the ranch for an extended visit? It will give both of y'all a chance to start the healing process. County air is good for things like healing."

"I'll think about it. Now let's go home so you can get some sleep." Putting the car into drive, I started the hour long journey back home.

**

Once Sasha was tucked snugly into bed, Blake and I sat on the sofa while the film "Never been kissed" played in the background. My eyes were not watching the television though. Instead they were focused at the brown haired cowboy sitting beside me.

He handed me another glass of wine and asked, "How are ya feeling really?"

I leaned my head back against the couch. I was exhausted both physically and emotionally.

"I'm not sure. I just feel…empty inside. It's like there is this black hole that is sucking my emotion away. I don't know how to explain it."

Tears started to flow from my eyes and down my cheeks. I tried to wipe them away so he wouldn't notice, but it was already too late.

"Darlin', one day you will look back and it won't hurt so much anymore. If you want, I'll be by your side every step of the way." His arms wrapped around me and I let myself fall to pieces. Sobbing on his shoulders, I felt safe in Blake's arms and I let myself fall into an exhausted sleep while he held me close.

Sometime later I was awakened by soft snoring in my ear. Turning my head around, I could see Blake behind me on the couch. His arms were wrapped tightly around me as if he was afraid to let go. I felt slightly uncomfortable and weird curled up with my best friend on the sofa, so I extracted myself from his arms. I placed a blanket across him as he slept. Flicking off the television, I quietly walked up the stairs to check on Sasha. Peering into her room, my throat tightened when I saw her curled up around one of her Father's jumpers. I could feel more tears cascading down my face once again. I didn't think I would ever stop crying. Using the door frame for support, I leaned against it as my heart broke even more for her loss. Footsteps behind me caused me to turn toward the sound, but I relaxed when I realized that Blake has followed me upstairs. Seeing my tears he placed his arm around my shoulder as he looked into Sasha's room. After closing her bedroom door, Blake took me into a hug without saying a word.

As his strong arms embraced me, I let my tears fall, but not before I could feel his own tears falling on my bare shoulder.

**

The next couple of days passed in a complete blur. With Blake's help I had managed to phone the funeral directors to arrange a cremation for Carl, book a place for a wake and get all my finances in order. Nonetheless, I still didn't feel comfortable in my own home. Everywhere I looked I could see reminders of Carl—from his jumper across the back of the chair to the mobile phone that the police had returned to me along with some other personal effects. These items were now sitting in a box on the table, waiting for me to go through them. But I was not ready to deal with them. Blake had helped me pack up Carl's clothes saying that if I left it too long I'll never do it. He was probably right about that. While it was hard, I managed to pack his clothes. We put them in three separate boxes. Keep. Donate. And dispose. Blake said that after the funeral he would take the boxes to the relevant places so I didn't have to do it. This way I could concentrate on grieving with Sasha.

Blake being here with us at this time was a miracle and he made my day-to-day business easier, especially when it came to Sasha. Blake would take Sasha out to the meadows to feed and pet the horses if I wasn't feeling up for it. It made me happy that he had come all this way to help me. I don't think I could have coped on my own these last couple of days if he hadn't been here. Now I could focus on what was happening today. It was now time to say a final goodbye to my husband, lover, and friend.

"Are y'all ready, Darlin?" Blake asked. "The car will be here any minute."

I was quietly sat at the kitchen table chain smoking. I did not want to be here today. I finished off my cup of coffee and stubbed out the cigarette in the overflowing ashtray. The car was due to pick us up in 5 minutes, but I was finding it a struggle to get myself moving. I didn't want to say goodbye to Carl, but I knew I had to do so soon. People would be offering me their sympathies and condolences and that made my skin crawl. I'm not a social person by nature so this was going to take every bit of willpower I had in me to get me through this day. I just wanted this day to end so I could drown my sorrows in a bottle of Jack.

Footsteps came up behind me and a hand was placed on my shoulder.

"Come on, Darlin', we need to get moving." Taking a deep breath I stood up and put on my shoes and coat.

"I'm ready," I replied with a long sigh before walking toward the waiting cars outside. My neighbours were already out by the front yard ready to pay their respects with bowed heads. This was going to be the longest day of my life…

Chapter 7

Being at the funeral was hard and it made me suddenly realize that I was now a widow at thirty six with a twelve year-old daughter. After hearing all the condolences from those who attended, my heart felt like it was breaking all over again. Every time someone said something nice about Carl, it was like losing another piece of my soul. People who he had worked with came to pay their respects. Some I knew and others I did not. But the one who made me cry the hardest was Sasha. She got up and told the other mourners about how much she loved her Daddy and how hard life would be without him. But she was lucky as she still had her Mama. The guy that crashed into her father could have just as easily crashed into her car as he drove past on the same stretch of road.

Blake took hold of my hand and I let myself cry. I lost who I believed was the love of my life. He was my soul mate and the father of my daughter. Despair filled me again at the realization that Carl would never see her graduate or walk her down the aisle or hold his first grandchild. Now I needed to be her Mum and her Dad and I really didn't know how I was going to do this alone.

Once the service was over we made our way down to the local pub where food and drinks would be served to anyone who wished to reminisce about the good times and the bad. Many stories were told about Carl and his wicked sense of humour. Carl was always the practical joker at work. No one ever knew if or when they were going to find a cringe-worthy picture from some long forgotten work party taped to their desk. That was my husband and his whole team respected and loved him. But now he was gone and a sombre atmosphere settled in the office. He was the one who made the work day a little lighter.

Taking Sasha in my arms, I led her away from the group of well-wishers and mourners so we could have some quiet mother-daughter time. That and I wanted to talk to her about maybe leaving the only home she knew in Wales and going to Uncle Pete's ranch. The ranch was a place where she could be with family. I didn't know if I was just being selfish, but I needed to get away. While I did love my home here, there were too many bad memories. First my parents were killed and then my husband. It was time for a fresh start.

"How are you doing, Dove?" I asked my little girl as she sobbed in my arms.

"Mum, can we go? I want to go home," she said, tears running down her cheeks.

"Yes, Flower, we can. Let me say my goodbyes and I'll ask Blake to drive us back." Seeing my daughter into the arms of her friend Kara and her parents, I made my way to the microphone the pub set up. I wanted to thank everyone for coming. Turning to the room I began to speak,

"I just wanted to say thank you to all who have come today to celebrate Carl's life. I've always known Carl was a very special person and that had been proven by all the love showed here today. Some people I know and some I don't, but I want to thank all of you. While Carl will be deeply missed by myself and Sasha as well as all of you, I know that he is looking down at us, encouraging us to all drink up and have one final soiree in his name. So let us raise a glass in memory to this wonderful father and husband. May we meet again someday. To Carl..." As the whole crowd echoed the toast, I took hold of Blake's arm and led him to where Sasha was sitting with Kara.

"Are you ready, Dove?" I asked taking her hand. She nodded her head sombrely. I helped her stand before walking out of the door to the awaiting car. While it was nice to say a final goodbye to Carl, I knew that my life would never be the same again. I had promised him that if anything ever happened to him I would never look at another man again. No one would ever compare to him.

Chapter 8

It had been two weeks since the funeral and life was starting to finally feel normal again. Blake had to return to the ranch due to my Uncle breaking his leg in a bad fall. Sasha had gone back to school and I was still on bereavement leave. I spent my days sorting out Carl's stuff and crying until I exhausted myself completely. The home that we built and had grown to love now felt like a prison. The bad memories had started to outweigh the good. Sasha didn't want to move because she said she had a life here. However, I needed to go back home and away from all this. There was a reason I needed to get away and back to the place I felt comfortable and loved. A week after the funeral, I found Carl's cell phone and out of nothing but a habit, I placed it on its charger. I don't know why I did it. Maybe it was fate.

**

Sat on the floor, I was going to go through some more of Carl's belongings when a knock on the door echoed around the empty house. Startled, I jumped and spilled the wine I was drinking on my clothes. "Great!" I mumbled to myself as I blotted the stain off my clothes. I got up, wondering who would be banging at my door this early in the day. I opened the front door and found a slim young woman standing there on the steps. She had bright blue eyes and dark ebony hair, but her eyes seemed haunted.

"Are you Mrs. Lewis?" she asked rather timidly while shifting on her feet.

"I am," I replied, not trying to hide my annoyance.

"I'm sorry to disturb you, but I needed to speak to you about your husband."

My heart clenched as well as my fists as I felt the emotion flood through my body. "My Husband is dead!" I practically shouted at the poor girl standing on my doorstep. The girl looked ready to run from my presence at any moment.

"I know, I'm sorry, but I needed to speak to you," she said, practically in a whisper. "Do you mind if I come in?" Taking a step back, I let her into the house.

"Come, follow me to the living room." I took a seat on the sofa and instructed her to sit down as well. "I recognize you. You were at the funeral."

The girl looked at me with frightened eyes. "Yes I was there," she stammered. "I didn't want to go, but I needed to see for myself that he was dead." I was on edge and the somewhat off the cuff statement made my blood boil. I must have looked as if I was about to explode like Mt. Vesuvius. Sensing my anger, she flinched and held her arms up to her face as if to block a blow. She actually thought I was going to slap her.

Reeling in my anger, I said, "I wasn't going to hit you." I took her hands and brought them down to place them in her lap. Looking at the girl, I could see the fear in her eyes as she lowered her hands. Suddenly she just burst into gut-wrenching sobs on my sofa.

"I'm sorry. It's just that he used to hit me. All the time. For no reason. I just got a little scared."

"Who hit you, sweetheart?" Hearing the calmer more motherly pitch of my voice she breathed a sigh of relief, but then thought maybe she might have made a mistake.

"Maybe I shouldn't have come." She stood up to leave, but I placed a firm, yet gentle hand on her arm.

"Sit, please. Who hit you?" I asked. Tears sprang into her eyes.

"Carl did. Carl used to hit me." Something ripped at my heart as the girl openly wept into her hands.

"Why on Earth would he hit you?" Giving her a tissue, I offered her a glass of wine to calm her nerves.

"We were dating for about 6 months roughly. I thought it was going well..."

"Wait, what?" I said, not believing I was hearing her right. But I stopped myself from going off the rails again and just let her speak.

"He told me you two were having marital problems and he didn't love you anymore. I've never been one to hook up with married men, but he was so nice and charming. You know the type. He wined and dined me until I would do anything for him. Suddenly there was a change in him. He would come over my house and start hitting me for no reason before having sex with me that was so rough it hurt." Feeling myself go pale, I sat back on the sofa and took a long sip of wine to calm my now frazzled nerves. "This went on for about four months. Then I found out he was seeing another woman in the office. Felicity Barnes. I had enough and I broke it off with him. He was so angry. Psychotic even. He beat me so bad that I had to be rushed to the hospital with several broken ribs and a broken wrist." She looked at me with a long stare and I knew she was telling the truth. She stood up and made her way to the door. "I'm sorry, but I thought you would want to know what kind of man he really was. I don't know if he beat you or anything, but I had heard mention from several women in the office that he was bad news. Be grateful, Mrs. Lewis. You had a lucky escape. If you don't believe me, look at his phone." Without any other word, she walked out of the door and vanished from sight.

Still stunned, I went and picked up his phone. It was fully charged. My stomach was in knots as I powered it on. As the screen lit up, Carl's phone came to life, chiming with dozens of incoming text messages. I never had a reason to read his messages. He always told me that he had some confidential material on his phone for work and not to touch his phone for any reason. I now wondered if that was a lie too. However, instead of turning off the phone, I looked at the messages from one of his female work colleagues. There was one dating back to the day of the crash. Before I knew it, I was reading the text messages between Carl and the girl called Felicity Barnes. I never knew just how close they were until now. I was such a fool. I started reading the messages dating back to one year.

[FB] "Thank you for last night. I'm glad that we had a chat. LMAO. If only I had known what we would end up doing after I told you how I felt about you, I would never have been so nervous."

[FB] "Carl, are you coming over tonight? I've got some new lingerie from Ann Summers that I know you will like."

[FB] "Wow, Carl I never knew you could do that in bed. Your wife is missing out. Give me a call so we can hook up."

The messages just kept getting dirtier and dirtier until the one sent before his crash.

[FB] "I know you don't want to hurt LJ. She is a sweetheart and so naïve, but come on babe, you know I can rock your world like no other. Isn't it time you finally left your wife so you and I can start our life together? I miss when you are not here warming my bed. I miss us fucking into the wee hours of the morning. How does LJ not know that you are actually hooking with me while on these business trips? Do you even love me? We are so good together, both in and out of the sack."

[CL] "Felicity love, I don't want to hurt LJ, we have been together for so long. But I stopped loving her years ago. Tonight I will tell her it is over, and we will finally get a chance to start our life together. You are my world now and the best lay I have ever had. That thing you do with your tongue when you are going down on me practically makes my toes curl. I'll call you tonight at about 9 pm so you know where to pick me."

[FB] "Carl, how did it go? You said you would call me but you never did, do you not want to see this perfect little pussy again. I'm waiting for your call. Love Felicity..."

Choking on my sobs, I threw the phone across the room. He had been cheating on me for a year, maybe even longer, and from what the strange girl with the black hair said it had been going on for much longer. Picking up our wedding album, I angrily threw it in a black trash bag and left it in the dustbin for the council to pick up in the morning. I also gave Claire a ring so she could keep me company with copious amounts of wine and chocolate until the small hours of the morning.

**

That night and every single night after, I cried myself to sleep. All those times he had told me that he loved me and would miss me while he was on his long business trip...it was a lie. A big fat juicy lie. He was actually with another woman. Touching and making love to another while I slept in an empty bed. How had I not seen it? How was I so blind? I knew I had put on weight since having Sasha, but not once had he called me on it or said he had stopped loving me. We still made love whenever he returned from his extended "business trips" and I even lost some of the weight, but obviously that hadn't been good enough. When I got up the nerve to look at the company website and at the people who worked with Carl, I found out that Felicity was a size ten Redhead, with legs that went on for days. She was very beautiful, with green eyes and a sexy little smirk that shined through the picture. It made me think she was probably having dirty thoughts as the photo was being taken. No wonder she had turned Carl's head. Just by her body language in the photo, she oozed sexuality. This was a person who was not afraid to try new things and experiment both in and out of the bedroom. It was then I decided I could not stay here any longer. My whole world was shattered.

**

A week had gone by since I discovered my marriage was a lie. I was packing up all of my belongings so it could go into storage. This was just temporary until I could figure out a way to get everything sent to Texas. Carl's life insurance had covered the mortgage leaving us with enough to live quite comfortably elsewhere. The realtor was coming around this morning to value the house for market. Claire said she would look after everything until a final sale. After thirteen years of marriage, we had accumulated a lot of creature comforts. Not all of it was coming with us. Because I was eager to leave, Claire said that she would have an estate sale so we could clear out what we no longer needed. For now, I booked the flights to Austin, Texas and got our passports and other paperwork together. Our suitcases were packed and with the clothes we would need for the warm weather in Texas and any personal items we put into the hand luggage. One of these personal items was my memory box full of the letters from Blake and a photo album of Sasha.

"Are you all packed up?" Claire asked. She had come to keep me company while I packed. Her husband Dave was out selling my car to the local garage, so I didn't t have to worry about that either. He would pick up Sasha and Kara and bring them home. I felt Sasha needed some time with her best friend. I promised her that Kara could come to visit her any time.

"I think that is everything. When Sasha gets home we will be ready to leave." Sat on the sofa, I pulled my knees up to my chest and let the tears flow. Claire perched on the edge of the seat next to me. When I started to cry again she took me in her arms.

"You know it is for the best, right? You will be with your family and maybe start your life again." Wiping away the tears on my face I shook my head at her remark.

"No, I promised Carl I would never look at another man again. Even though he broke his promise to be faithful to me, I would never go back on my promises."

Claire shook her head in dismay. "You are an idiot."

I looked up at her in shock. "Sorry?"

"Look," she said, holding me at arm's length and looking me in the eyes. "I didn't mean to call you an idiot. But really, after what he did? He had the nerve to demand that of you. You shouldn't have to live the rest of your life as a nun... That's so Carl. Selfish even in death. I'm sorry I have to be the one to knock some sense into you."

"Claire, I'm just not ready."

"I don't mean to say you should jump in the sack with the next red-blooded male you see. Give yourself time to mourn and then get back out there. You are still a young and very beautiful woman. You need to get back out there and find someone who will love you for you."

I smiled at my friend. "I'll take your advice under consideration." I heard the front door open and saw Dave, Sasha, and Kara enter the house. The two girls had tear tracks running down their faces. I felt bad for separating them, but there was no turning back now. "Are you ready, Dove?" She nodded her head and wiped the tears from her face. Nodding my head to Dave, he picked up our suitcases and hand luggage and took them to the car. With one final check, I made sure that I had the passports, money, and documents we would need to make a fresh start in America.

Then I took Sasha's hand and locked the door for the last time before handing over the keys to Claire.

"Will anyone be meeting you when you get off of the plane, LJ?" Dave asked as he closed the lid of the boot.

Shaking my head, I looked at him before getting into the car. "Nope, I didn't tell them I was coming," I said before closing the car door. Dave thumped the roof of the car and we drove off, leaving behind our old life to begin a new one.

Chapter 9

The heat enveloped me immediately, sweat running down my body, once we left the sanctuary of the airport's air conditioning. While Wales was beautiful, Texas had a certain charm, with its flat landscapes that go on as far as the eye could see. The warm, dry air made my breath catch in my throat. Sasha wasn't feeling her best either.

"Mama, it's too hot here," Sasha whined as she dragged her suitcase toward the exterior of the airport.

"You will get used to it, Dove." Taking hold of her hand we walked in the direction of the metro station, we still had a way to go.

"Where are we going?" She sounded tired and irritated,

"We have to get on a Greyhound bus for our final leg of the journey. So, my darling, we are walking to the depot."

"How long will it take us to get to Uncle Pete's ranch, Mama?" She asked as we climbed aboard the metro bus that has just arrived at the terminal. This was Sasha's version of *Are we there yet?*

I sighed, trying not to sound like I was getting annoyed myself. It had been a long journey and we were both exhausted. "Not long now,

Dove. Once we get to the Greyhound station we can catch another bus which will drop us a couple of miles from the ranch's gates.'"

"So, you are saying we're going to have to walk even more?" she grumbled, taking her seat.

After stowing our bags, I sat next to her. "Trust me, Dove, it will be worth all this bother. I'm sure you will love it and forget all about your sore feet."

"What's the ranch's name, Mama?" she asked me again for what seems like the hundredth time.

"Coyote Lodge, Sweetheart."

She looked suddenly frightened. "Are there coyotes there?"

"Don't worry about them. There are more afraid of you then you are of them, Now hush, Dove, I've not caught a bus in such a long time. I need to try and remember what bus we need to take." I pulled out a bunch of Greyhound schedules and started to study them. Finding it I point out the number coach we need to take. "See this one drives straight past the ranch.

After about a half an hour, we got off the Metro and walked into the Greyhound station. I walked over to the ticket counter and bought two one way tickets. When I got back to Sasha she was sat on her suitcase.

"Why didn't you phone Blake so he could come and get us, Mama? He wouldn't have minded." Crossing her arms, she glared at me from over her sunglasses.

"Because I didn't tell them we were coming?"

"Why not?"

"I wanted it to be a surprise."

"Ohhh."

"I'll be fun, I promise."

**

The journey on the bus was very pleasant, especially since the driver had the air conditioning cranked up to the maximum. However, it wasn't long before I could see our stop on the horizon. The driver called out the next stop.

"Come on, Dove, it won't be long now. Soon we can rest, but we need to get off at this stop." I pressed the call button and helped Sasha up and wheeled both our cases towards the front of the bus.

"Are y'all sure this is where ya wanna get off here, little lady?" the bus driver asked in a deep southern drawl as he slowed the bus to a stop. "There isn't much around for miles." Smiling I placed my hand on his shoulder and said, "Yes, there is. Coyote Lodge is not far from here."

He nodded his head and pulled up to the stop so he could let Sasha and I off the bus. Being a southern gentleman, he helped with the luggage. I thanked him and offered a tip, but he just tipped his hat and got back on the bus. The bus drove off and I could feel my heart lift slightly. I was finally happy at being at the only other place I would gladly call home.

"Come on, Dove we still have a way to go yet."

Sasha groaned in a way only a pre-teen could. Ensuring that both sides of the dusty road were clear of on coming traffic, we crossed the road and started walking.

**

"Mama, tell me more about when you were a kid growing up?" My daughter had been peppering me with questions ever since we got off the bus. I could tell that her feet were hurting from the long walk on the hard, compacted road. But she was a trooper.

"Well, your grandparents used to bring me out here every year to spend summer with Uncle Pete. We always had so much fun. One year Uncle Pete taught me how to round up stray cattle who had wandered off his pastures. We would spend hours on horseback looking for those silly cows. One year when we were riding back to the ranch while pushing the lost cows toward home, a rattlesnake spooked my horse. Horses do not like snakes in general, but rattlesnakes—well because of their tail warning system—it freaks horses like you wouldn't believe. My horse reared up and threw me from the saddle. Damn near broke my arm. She bolted and I was left in a cloud of dust with a pain you wouldn't believe."

"What happened next, Mama?" she asked wide eyed.

"Well, while Uncle Pete was tending to my arm and making a sling from his bandanna, all the cows decided to run away again. Oh, he was furious. I never heard his curse so much."

"He was angry you got hurt?"

"Not at all. He was angry because the snake spooked the horse and almost killed me. Uncle Pete cusses a lot when he gets emotional. Got to keep up that tough cowboy appearance, you know."

"Men," she groaned.

Laughing, I continued, "As I was sitting there in pain and he was swearing up a storm, this young kid comes riding up with his cowboy hat and boots. He was smirking and looking down at me. Then the little smart mouth says, "Maybe y'all should learn to hold on to your horse before rustling Beeves." My Uncle turned his swearing from me to the young lad, "My niece can ride better than y'all any day. Like to see what ya would do if you came across rattler. Probably soil your diapers, boy."

"What is that...beeves?" Sasha asked as she took a sip of her water. "I've never heard that word before." I smiled and placed my free arm around her shoulder.

"It's what Texans call cows." As she laughed I carried on with the story. "Well, the boy looks at me and says, "Well if ya ever want to prove your Uncle right my name is Blake and I will gladly show ya how a cowboy can ride. He was always cocky in that charming kind of way."

"Is that how you met Blake? Did you prove him wrong?"

Ruffling her hair with my free hand I let out a laugh, "I sure did, Dove, your mama showed that young buck that even with a broken arm I could outrun him on a horse. From that day on, we remained firm friends even though he was three years younger than I am." Pulling her to the side of the road, I sat down on a rock and patted the seat next to me. "Look around Dove what do you see?"

Scrunching up her eyes Sasha looked around the surrounding area. "I see fields of dry grasses and not much else." Satisfied with her answer she attempted to stand up but I pulled her back down to sit next to me.

"Now, Dove, close your eyes and listen to the surrounding sounds." I did the same and closed my eyes to take in the alien world around me.

"I hear the grass swishing, Mama, but it is so different from home. Back home you can tell when the rain has soaked the ground by the sound of the grass moving, it is slow and deep. But here it sounds dry and brittle like a grass skirt the women wear in Hawaii."

Smiling, I looked at her, but not before hearing the sound of approaching horse hooves. "What else do you hear, Dove?"

She scrunched up her eyes as if it would help her hear better and held her breath until she let it out in a gasp. "I can hear a horse," she said looking around for it. She finally spotted a lone rider in the distance. "There!" she said, pointing.

I looked to where she was pointing and saw the silhouette of a man on horseback. I would know that form anywhere. It was Blake. He was probably checking the property and spotted us in the distance. That man had the eyesight of an eagle. As he got closer, his eyes lit up in delight once he realized it was us.

"LJ, Sasha!" he exclaimed before jumping off of his horse and gathering us in his strong arms. "What! What are y'all doing here? Why didn't ya tell us y'all were coming? I would've met ya at the airport."

"See, Mama, I told you."

"Yes, you did, sweetheart. But this is much better." Smiling I hugged him back and breathed deep, taking in the smell of horses and hay. "I wanted to surprise everyone."

"Well, Darlin' ya certainly surprised me. That's for sure." Grabbing our bags, he pulled a rope from his saddle horn and secured the bags to the back of the horse. As if she weighed nothing, he picked up Sasha and placed her on his horse. "Now you are a real cowgirl," he said to Sasha. She blushed and smiled. He was such a charmer. He took the reins in one hand and my free hand in his other. Our fingers were entwined and I felt like I was finally home. "Let's get y'all home now. Your Uncle will be happy as pigs in shit ta see ya."

"Okay, ew," Sasha said as he led us down the dusty road.

**

"So how long are y'all staying for?" Blake asked as he put a blanket across Sasha's shoulders to keep her warm. The temperature dropped quickly once the sun went down.

"For good I hope. Of course that is if Uncle Pete will have us." As he placed his hand on my shoulder to give me a gentle squeeze, I felt little bolts of electricity running through my body. The contact and my reaction shocked me to my core. The only other time I had felt like this was when I met Carl. One look from Carl would turn my legs to jelly and my heart rate sky-rocket. However, I knew that nothing would ever happen between Blake and me for two reasons. Firstly, Blake was my oldest friend in the world and secondly, I made a promise to Carl that if anything ever happened to him I would not look at another man. While that promise would be hard, I knew in my heart that it was one promise I would have to keep. Besides, Blake was a 33-year-old single, red-blooded male, while I was a frumpy, overweight 36-year-old widow with a nearly teenage daughter. What would he want with me? A woman whose husband had cheated on her more than once. Why would someone as good-looking at Blake look twice at me when he had his choice of any Texan beauty? Taking a minute to shake myself from my mental thoughts I decided there and then that I would keep my promise to Carl and not hook up with any other man.

Chapter 10

"Hey, little Darlin', are ya falling asleep on that horse?" Blake asked, shaking Sasha's leg lightly as her head started to drop toward her chest. Laughing he pulled her from the horse so he could carry her to the ranch which was at the end of the driveway. This left me to taking the reins of his horse before she had the chance to wander off.

"How is everyone, Blake? It's been so long since I've seen them all." I started to play with the mane of the horse out of nervousness. I don't know why I was feeling nervous. It was only Blake after all.

"Your Uncle is fine apart from acting like a bear with a sore head because he can't work the ranch while his leg is a cast. My Ma and Pa moved further into Austin. Pops had a heart attack a few years ago. Remember I wrote ya about it?" I nodded my head and he continued. "Well they asked if I wanted the family ranch, but I was just starting to hit the big time in the rodeo. I didn't want the burden. Selfish, I know. I kind of wished I had bought the ranch off of them. I'm thirty three. I should be thinking about settling down at my age. But the Rodeo is in my blood."

As we continued the walk up the path, suddenly, I saw the homestead ahead of me. I smiled at the vison. It looked exactly as I remembered. The home was made of weathered wood and had two floors with a wraparound porch. I could see the red and white checked curtains that my Auntie had made long time ago, hanging in the windows. Above the doorframe, as tradition dictated in these parts, was a horseshoe with the prongs pointing up to signify good luck to all who entered. On the outside of the porch, I could see a statue that I remembered making as a child with all the Native American arrowheads I had found on the land over the years.

"I can't believe he kept that thing outside where everyone can see," I said, pointing at the statue I had made when I was fourteen. I did have Blake's help at the time. So technically it was a team effort.

"Well Darlin', it is his pride and joy. Do ya remember how we would spend days on end looking for all those arrow heads? Hell, sometimes we didn't even make it home before dark. We had to camp out under the stars with just our riding blankets."

Flushing at the memory I smiled at him. "Wasn't it one of those nights when you told me you were going to marry me?" Changing my voice I try to imitate what Blake said to me in his pre-teen voice. "LJ, my Darlin', one-day y'all forget I'm three years younger than ya and let me sweep ya off your feet." I nudged him with my shoulder and he laughed.

"Well ya were my first crush. I was determined to marry ya when I was older. That was the night before y'all left and never came back. Damn near broke my heart, Darlin' when ya refused to come back to the ranch. Every summer I would wait by those gates for the bus, but ya never came back." As we reached the porch, I tied the horse to the post and watched as Blake placed Sasha gently on the bench outside the front door. He tucked the blanket around her, but she was fast asleep and didn't even move. Turning to me he waited for me to join him on the porch. He took my hand in his and raised it to his lips. "When I was twenty and ya married Carl, I realized that y'all were never going to come back to me." He placed his hand on my cheek and gently rubbed it with his thumb. "I never forgot ya though. Every time y'all wrote me, I would remember every single world."

Sighing, I placed my hand on his and took off of my cheek. "And look what you would have ended up with. A woman older than you who is overweight. I'm no longer a spring chicken. Even Carl stopped finding me attractive." Tears ran down my cheek, but Blake brushed them away.

"That's bull! How can ya say that? You are a beautiful woman with a gorgeous daughter. Carl loved ya with every breath of his being. He even wrote to me to tell me to stop all correspondence with you. He said when you got my letters, he could see how upset you got. How your eyes would get all misty and he couldn't get five words out of you."

Staring at him, I laughed at what he has just said. "Yeah, well, I doubt he loved me all that much. He had been having affairs behind my back up until the day he died. He told these women that he had fallen out of love with me years ago." Turning away from him, I placed my hands on the porch railing to steady myself as my heart broke in two again. Suddenly I felt strong arms reaching around me to hold me tight.

"Well he was a dang fool. He had a beautiful woman who loved him with every fibre of her being. The fact he threw that all away for a quick roll in the hay makes him a crazy person." Leaning back, I settled my back into his arms, "Why did y'all never come back?"

Standing up from my slouch I sigh audibly. "After my parents died I didn't know what I wanted to do. I nearly came home, but then I met Carl and I knew that I could never come home. Plus you were starting to live your own life and touring the rodeos with your father. When I got married I thought you would forget about me. You were living your life and I didn't want to come and disrupt it. But I did keep every letter you sent."

He turned me around with surprise in his eyes. "Y'all kept every single one?" Nodding I give him a little shove. "Even the presents I sent you?" I grinned at him, lifting my shirt and showing off the belt buckle I finally managed to wrestle back from Sasha. Just as he was about to say something the door opened and my Uncle Pete was standing there. More like being propped up by his crutches. Uncle Pete's hair was a silvery white and his blue eyes stood out from his tanned, weather worn features.

"I thought I heard voices. Welcome home sweetheart." Immediately I'm swept out of Blake's embrace and into the arms of my Uncle whom I haven't seen since he gave me away at the wedding.

"Uncle Pete, you are looking well...except for the broken leg."

"Your room is all made up?" Shock and confusion settled on my face. "How? How did you know?

"Claire phoned me to let me know y'all were on the way. Ya have a good friend there." He led me into the homestead leaving Blake to carry Sasha from the bench into the house. She started to stir after hearing my Uncles loud, booming voice. Startled she looked around when she realized that Blake was carrying her.

"Did I fall asleep mama?"

Nodding at her I watched as Blake took her up the stairs. "It's alright, Dove, just go back to sleep."

"Put her in LJ's old room," Uncle Pete shouts after him. "I thought I would give her your old room. Constance came and aired it out for y'all.

Got you all new linens. Here have a seat. I bet you are tired from the journey." He led me to the seat and I glanced around the home in awe. My Uncle had been on his own for a few years yet I noticed that there were traces of a woman's touch around the house.

"Who's Constance?" I asked. He placed a fatherly arm across my shoulders.

"She is my girl. She was a godsend to me after Auntie Clara passed. She said she will pop by tomorrow to see you." Smiling, he gave me a gentle shake. "You need to go and sleep, I bet you are plum tired."

"I'll go up shortly, Uncle. You get to bed and rest that leg I'm going to have a smoke before I hit the sheets."

He kissed my head and then moved to the foot of the stairs. He paused for a moment and said, "I'm glad y'all home Sweetheart. I've missed ya." With watery eyes, he made his way up to his room. I went outside and sat on the bench. I lit a cigarette and took a deep drag. Closing my eyes I tried to relax. Suddenly a red afghan blanket was placed around my shoulders. Blake sat next to me and took my hand in his.

"Those things will kill ya, Darlin'," he said, removing the cigarette from my hand to take a drag from it.

"You shouldn't be smoking, Blake. Aren't you supposed to be fighting fit for the rodeo?"

"One drag every now and then won't hurt," he said, pulling me back into his arms. "So tell me, why did y'all never bring Carl to visit the ranch or Uncle Pete?"

Taking a deep breath, I knew I would get asked this eventually. But how could I tell him that Carl was a jealous man. So jealous in fact that he said he would rather not meet Blake at all. "We just never had the money. Living pay check to pay check just about killed us financially," I lied. He nodded his head, but I could tell by the raised eyebrow that he didn't believe me one bit. However, instead of calling me on it, he just sat there quietly holding me while we listened to the sounds of the night surrounding us. Looking up I noticed how the sky was full of stars until it appeared that an ocean of lights were above our heads. "I've forgotten what the stars look like out here!" Sat in the arms of a cowboy, we watched the fireflies dance in the sky among the stars I finally felt a sense of peace and of being home. I don't know how long we were sitting there, but eventually the jet lag caught up with me and my face broke into a jaw-splitting yawn.

"Come on, Darlin', time for bed," Blake said as he pulled me up from the bench into his waiting arms. "You are nearly dead on your feet.

Get yourself in that house and into bed. I'll see ya in the morning." Staring at him I could feel the tension build as I realized how close we were until he kissed me lightly on the lips. "Good night, sweetheart," he said before walking off into the night. I ran back into the house and leaned against the closed door. My face was flushed red. I lifted hand up to my cheeks. What just happened? Did Blake just kiss me? Why am I acting like a school girl? I felt a slight grin on my face. I shook the feeling and then just walked quietly up the stairs to my bedroom.

Chapter 11

"Mama, can I go and see the horses?" Sasha asked, jumping onto the top of my bed and jostling me awake. I was in the middle of a dream. But this one was peaceful. I hadn't dreamed like that in a while. The peaceful ones had returned to me because I was finally able to have a night of uninterrupted sleep. Sasha's brown eyes stared at me and they were full of wonder and excitement. "Uncle Pete said I could if you were okay with it?"

Smiling at my daughter I rubbed my hand over her head before I pulled her in for a big hug. "Of course you can, Dove." She let out a yell of pleasure and ran out of my room calling out to Uncle Pete.

"Mama said it was okay!" she squealed, running down the hall.

I tried to pull myself out of the sleep driven fog. We had been here nearly a week and I was pleased to see that instead of wallowing in the fact she had left her best friend behind, Sasha was thriving on the ranch. She had been getting up earlier than I had ever seen her do. Just to help Blake with the horses. At the crack of dawn he would take her around the property to show her the ins and outs of daily working life on a ranch. He did the same exact thing when we were kids and he was helping my Uncle.

It made my heart grow, knowing that he was there to keep my daughter entertained and busy while her Mama was slowly falling apart.

Admittedly, I often found myself staring off into space, remembering the soft kiss Blake bestowed upon me the night we arrived. I was immediately filled with guilt that I actually enjoyed it. I knew deep down that I shouldn't have even thought of kissing another, especially since my husband had only been gone for a month. Did that make me a bad person? Carl had made me promise that if anything had ever happened to him I would never replace him with another man. I could already feel that little space in my heart which held a piece of Blake start to grow. Maybe Claire was right? Or maybe I was just looking for an excuse. No, no, I made a promise. Shaking these thoughts from my mind, I climbed out of bed, cleaned up and headed downstairs to see if my Uncle needed help around the home.

Not surprisingly, Uncle Pete was not around. However, sat at the table was his girl Constance. When I met her a week ago I was unsure of how I would react but I quickly realized that she was an amazing woman. She had Native American colouring and she looked absolutely stunning for her age. But it was her eyes that drew me to her. They were the kindest I had ever seen. Most people who had brown eyes could look a bit stern, but hers had a light in them. Her eyes held a bit of mischief. Sasha had immediately taken a liking to her and they often spent their days making dream catchers or drawing horses. When it's just the two of us, we would sit over coffee and talk about my feelings. She would make a damn fine psychologist. My Uncle certainly had good taste in women. However, Constance was completely different from my Auntie. Aunt Clara had fine, short blonde hair and icy blue eyes. Constance on the other hand had thick, long black hair with streaks of grey that look like someone had put glitter in her hair. Her eyes were dark brown and held so much warmth in them that you couldn't help but feel you were the only person in the world.

"Morning, Honey," she said. Her thick Texan accent flowed over my skin as she got up to pour me a coffee. "Did you sleep well last night?" Taking a seat at the table, she handed me a gigantic cup coffee with just the right amount of milk and sugar in it.

"I did thank you. I haven't slept that well in ages. What was in that pillow you gave me?"

She tapped her nose knowingly.

The morning I had met Constance she remarked on how tired I looked. This led to a big discussion about herbs and their different healing properties. Last night she handed me a pillow that smelled faintly of Lavender and said it would help me sleep better.

"Well, Lavender mostly. But there were a few other herbs in there that will help to calm your mind so you can sleep better." Leaning against the counter she looked at me over the top of her coffee mug. "It also promotes good dreams. Don't think I haven't heard you screaming bloody murder in your sleep."

Taking a sip of my coffee I sighed. "It's just that I can't get the image of Carl like that…you know dead. I can't get it out of my head. In my dreams everything is in technicolour. Knowing it really did happen isn't helping me. Hopefully after that good sleep last night my bad dreams might ease off a bit." After thanking her for the coffee, I picked up my cup and sat out on the porch. I needed a cigarette to take the edge off. I really didn't want to talk about my dreams. If I did the nightmares might come back.

**

As the nicotine and caffeine worked its magic waking me up, I ran a hand across my face. I had slept without any bad dreams, but I still felt exhausted. I still couldn't cope with the changes that had happened in my life. It had only been a month and I was no better. I was starting to think it would never get any better. First my husband got killed in a car crash. He was the one person I thought I would spend the rest of my life with. Then I found out that my husband no longer loved me and was having affairs behind me back. Blindsided was a word that came to mind. And finally, every time I caught sight of my oldest friend in the world, my heart would beat harder in my chest. My cheeks would flush in excitement, giving me away. You'd think I was a teenager again.

My husband had been dead a month and I had started to notice someone else. I should be ashamed. This did not mean that I never loved my husband. Maybe it was the fact that finding out that my husband no longer loved me made me realize that I had been missing out on something. Something more pure. Why was I wasting my life with a man who no longer loved me when I could have had the brown-eyed cowboy who had been in my life since childhood? As these thoughts swirled around my mind like the cigarette smoke floating above my head, I felt confused. Where my thoughts were heading? I was in desperate need of a distraction. I got up from the porch and walked around the building to clear my mind. Without realising it, I followed the sounds of someone chopping wood.

And there he was. Blake. Blake there with his shirt off. Yum. *Stop it!* I thought to myself. He was preparing the logs for the fireplace. I didn't want to get caught leering at him so I leaned against the corner of the building so I could inconspicuously watch him as he worked. His arms looked so strong and sexy as he swung the axe and his tight abs showed a light sheen of sweat from his hard labour. I had never seen Blake with his shirt off before and my mind started to wander to a place I was sure would get me sent to hell.

I imagined running my fingers through his hair while we passionately kissed, his body fitting to me perfectly. From where I stood, or ogling as the case may be, I could see the dark thatch of hair in the middle of his chest. I followed the trail of fine hairs down his washboard stomach toward that forbidden place in my mind. Oh how I would like to run my fingers down the trail, feeling the softness of the fine hairs that would lead me further into the unknown. Biting my lip, I could feel lust rising in me. *Down, Girl!* Was my previous life so incomplete that just taking a glance at this cowboy sent my libido into overdrive? I've never been a very passionate woman, but in this instance the fire in my groin burned deep and made me realize that something was missing. Missing in my marriage. Missing in my life in general. Sexual equality. It took me until now to realize that my husband was a sadist who didn't care if he hurt me. It was all about his pleasure. Seeing Blake with his muscular arms and long fingers I could imagine what he would make sure the woman was satisfied before taking his own pleasure. I hadn't realized that I had groaned so loudly from my fantasy until Blake looked up and caught my eye. He grinned in that annoyingly sexy way and all I could do was duck around the corner of the house. My face flared with embarrassment.

Oh, my God, I'm such a wanton woman, I thought to myself as I held a hand to my cheek. I couldn't help but laugh at the stupidity of standing there like an idiot. It was almost as if I was a teenager again and I was seeing my crush naked for the first time. Mortified, I heard footsteps approaching from around the corner. Instead of waiting so I could laugh it off with him, I ran away toward the barn. Maybe grooming the horses would calm the raging inferno that was my libido.

**

Blake never did find me in the barn and I was grateful. It gave me a chance to cool down and stop acting like a lovesick, horny teenager. I thought I was well past the hormonal stages of my life. Facing facts, I brushed the horse in front of me with vigour as I realized that nothing could ever happen between Blake and myself. For one thing, he was three years younger than me and my oldest friend. Besides he had the pick of the litter. All those girls who hung around his were tall, blonde, skinny cowgirls. They were certainly not frumpy thirty six year olds who were overweight and whose dead husband didn't even find her attractive anymore.

"Good horse. Let me clean your hooves out now," I said in a calm voice to the bay mare in front of me. I picked up the horse shoe pick in one hand and attempted to lift her back leg with the other. She, however, had other ideas and refused to move her foot so I could clean out the mud that had caked itself in her shoe. "Oh, so it's going to be like that, huh?" With a grunt, I tried stroking her withers and cajole her to pull up the leg. Instead I ended up falling on my arse when she moved and knocked me over. Trying to stop my fall with my hand, I ended up impaling it on the sharper end of the pick. The sharp end cut right into the palm of my right hand.

"Fuck!" I shouted when the pain shot up my arm. I took the rag that I had been using to wipe off perspiration that accumulated while I was mucking out the horses' stalls. I pressed the rag onto the cut to stop the bleeding. It bloody hurt like hell. I tried to stand up and had to lean against the horse as a wave of dizziness came over me. I noticed that the blood was starting to soak through the rag.

I've never been good around blood especially my own. Squeamish was an understatement. When Sasha injured herself it was Carl who was the one who cleaned her wounds. Even the sight of a little blood was enough to make me end up on the floor next to her.

"Please don't let me faint. Please don't let me faint," I said in a mantra, trying to will myself. Unsteadily, I made my way to the stall door so I could sit on the bale of hay. I needed to calm my frazzled nerves. However, before I was anywhere near the stall door my equilibrium shifted and I stumbled to the ground. I was on the verge of passing out when I heard heavy footsteps approaching from outside the barn door.

**

He hadn't seen much of LJ since she had come back to Texas. She seemed to be avoiding him. He did however spend a lot more time with Sasha and the little girl was growing on him. It felt like he had his own daughter. It was cute the way she followed him around the ranch, trying to learn all about the lifestyle so she could help him. At the moment though, Sasha was helping her Great Uncle repair one of the fences so Blake was on his own to chop firewood for the homestead. As he entered the barn, he heard Bertha whinnying and stamping her feet from the stall. Immediately he thought that a varmint had gotten into the barn again and was spooking her. Dropping his armful of wood he turned the corner to see the bay mare frantic as she tried to get out of her stall. The door was wide open, but luckily she was tethered to the post.

"Shh, Darlin', what's got ya in a tizzy?" he asked the mare as he entered the stall to calm her nerves. He noticed the bloodied hoof pick on the ground by her feet. Worried that she might have hurt herself. He quickly checked her over for any wounds. Puzzled that he was no trace of blood on the horse he picked up the hoof pick and secured the stall. Turning to leave he spotted LJ on the ground with a bloodied rag tied around her hand. Rushing to her side, he shook her in an attempt to wake her. "LJ, honey, hey, are ya all right?"

Her eyes started to flutter open and he helped her sit up. "Oh, my head," she murmured.

"LJ, sweetheart, I need to look at your hand." Gently he removed the rag and opened her hand to inspect the damage. He soon started to worry when he saw the sweat on her brow and white complexion. The angry cut seems to scream at him as blood dripped steadily from the gash on her palm.

"Blake," she mumbled. She looked at her hand and started to swoon again. Her eyes started to roll back into her head when as she saw the blood.

"No, Darlin', don't ya go passing out on me again. I know I make the ladies swoon, but this is ridiculous," he said, trying to make light of the situation and keep her calm. "Come, on, we need to get this cut cleaned and stitched." He helped her stand back up while keeping her arm elevated as they made their way back to the house at a painfully slow pace.

Getting her to the house was not an easy task. Every so often she would stumble and nearly fall to the ground, but his strong grip on her body kept her upright. He would pick her up if he had to, but in the end they made it to the house. In order to stop her from looking at the blood steadily dripping down towards her elbow and fainting again, he pushed her face into his neck while keeping a steady pressure on the wound. Stumbling onto the porch he helped her sit on the bench before running into the house to grab the first aid kit.

"Where is the first aid kit?" he asked Constance who was sitting at the kitchen table.

Seeing the young cowboy's hurried expression, Constance stared at him for a moment and then pointed to a cabinet. He quickly explained that LJ had cut her hand on the hoof pick and he needed to treat it before it became infected. Grabbing the first aid kit, he checked the supplies and then ran back outside to LJ.

**

Holding myself upright on the bench I tried not to look at the wound while keeping pressure on it. Blake ran into the house to get the first aid kit. I knew that as soon as I caught sight of the blood again I was going to either pass out or throw up. I am such a wuss. As the door of the house opened I looked in that direction, but caught sight of the blood dripping down my arm. Already I could feel my vision starts to swim and nausea rolling in my stomach. Swallowing, I tried to concentrate on my breathing as Blake's calloused hand turned my head so that I was looking directly into his caring brown eyes.

"Just focus on me, Darlin', not on what I'm doing, okay?" Blake said. "Who knew you were such a girl, LJ," he teased while he took my hand to clean the wound with antiseptic. I concentrated on his frown lines while he was tending to my hand. It was a good distraction from the burning sensation in my hand. Without realizing it, I took my other hand and smooth my fingers along his brow trying to even out the frown lines. Startling him, he looked at me before he carried on cleaning my hand.

"Sorry," I said, immediately taking my hand away from his head.

"No, sweetheart, it's okay. If it means y'all won't pass out again then do whatever ya need to distract yourself." Smiling, I let my free hand trace itself down the side of his cheek towards his well-defined shoulders before trailing my nails down his chest. Before I even knew it, my fingers were tangled in the thick thatch of chest hair. My fingernails caught on one of his pert nipples. He shivered and I pulled my hand away.

What was I doing? The inferno inside me started to grow into epic proportions. Wincing I could feel the sting as he closed the wound on my palm. I placed my head on his shoulder, making sure that my nose was resting by his neck. Breathing in deep, I could smell the musky scent of sweat and horses. It wasn't an unpleasant scent and it certainly took my mind off the injury.

"We will have to keep an eye on this. It is only superficial, but any sign of infection and I'm taking y'all to the hospital," he said, breathing into my ear causing goose bumps to erupt on my skin.

"Thank you..." My voice sounded husky as I laid my head on his shoulder. "I can't believe I passed out. You're right, I am such a girl." As his shoulders shook with laughter I felt a smile appear on my lips.

"Don't worry, Darlin', if ya passed out I would've carried ya to the house. I've done it before remember" I lifted my head up and realized our lips were barely a breath apart.

"Ah, yes, I do."

The rodeo was coming up and I wanted to show that I could barrel race with the best of them. However that day I could not concentrate. I thought of the 14-year-old lad who had given up his time to help me look for arrowheads to finish that statue. That summer I had felt quite alone after Auntie Clara died. We were very close, but now I felt like a gaping hole was in my soul. Seeing how upset I was, Blake had taken me riding and showed me where he had found a load of new arrowheads. He told tall tales about the varmint he caught with his bare heads and other adventures. Not concentrating on what I was doing, I misjudged the last barrel causing my horse Peggy to buck and throw me straight into the fence. It cracked from the violence of the impact. I felt a searing pain in my leg and saw that one of the iron nails had punctured me. Blood was gushing out of the nasty wound. As darkness started to envelope me, Blake rode up, and even at fourteen years old, he towered over me. His years of working the ranch had left him with a body close to that of a pro wrestler. Picking me up as if I weighed nothing at all, he carried me to the house where my Uncle called an ambulance to take me to the hospital….

"Would you have really carried me?" I asked.

Smiling he places a hand against my cheek. "Always, Darlin'," he replied and leaned in to kiss me. He probably would have too, if Sasha hadn't comes running up the steps with Uncle Peter behind her.

"Mama, quick, you need to come with me." Jumping away from Blake, I looked at Sasha and saw the excitement in her eyes.

"What is it, Dove?"

She opened her mouth to speak and then noticed Blake wrapping a bandage around my hand. "What happened, Mama?" she asked touching my arm. "Did you hurt yourself?"

Nodding my head I used my free hand to pull her in for a hug. "A little cut is all. Why do you need me to come with you sweetie pie?"

Beaming, she grabbed my hand to pull me up. "Blake bought me a horse. I'm going to name her Meadow." Shocked, I stood still and looked between my daughter, who was grinning a hundred-watt smile and Blake, who suddenly found packing away the first aid kit very interesting.

With raised eyebrows, I said, "You bought her a horse?"

"Well...yeah." He rubbed the back of his neck like a nervous boy. "I thought since y'all were here for good she would be needing to practise her riding and all. She needs to make a bond with her own horse. Bertha is good, but she is a rodeo horse. Sasha needs a trekking horse." He sounded worried that I would be upset. Instead I gave him a quick kiss on the cheek.

"Thank you. I can't believe you bought her a horse though. I'll pay you for her."

Blake just shook his head. "No, it is a gift. She needs a horse and I do quite enjoy having the little cowgirl following me around and learning about ranch life." Removing his hat, he placed it on Sasha's head. "Now ya look like a little cowgirl." She laughed and ran off with his hat toward the barn.

"You know you are never going to see that hat again?" I stated, nudging him with my shoulder. I started laughing as he ran his fingers through is hair to fluff up the flat strands.

"I know but she is worth it," he said, smiling at me before heading after Sasha.

"He likes you, you know," My Uncle said to me out of nowhere. He had been watching our exchange from the railing.

"We've know each other for years. Of course he likes me," I responded dismissively.

"No, LJ, honey that is not what I mean and you know it. He has had a bee in his britches for you since he was a kid."

Standing next to my Uncle, I watched as Blake led Sasha out on a gorgeous chestnut coloured horse. "Don't be silly, Uncle. He doesn't. He can have his pick from a gaggle of women. I doubt I am his type."

He squeezed my shoulder gently and said, "Y'all keep telling yourself that. I know how that young man's mind works. That boy has got it bad for you."

Leaving me to contemplate all the facts, he walked back into the house. I watched Blake teaching Sasha how to ride properly. He was a natural and it seemed so was she. The truth of the matter was, I had it bad for him too, but I could never tell him.

Chapter 12

"Look Mama I'm riding!" Sasha yelled from atop her horse. I was sat on the fence watching her ride without a care in the world. It did my heart good to see that she was forgetting all of her troubles. Blake pulled her to the side and pointed toward me. She giggled and they both rode their horses over to me. I noticed the mischief on their faces and I leapt off the fence, taking a few paces back.

"And where do ya think ya going, Darlin'?" Blake teased, pulling his lasso from the saddle horn, "Ya know I can catch ya, right?" I watched as he swung the rope in the air and I tried to escape, but I found myself roped up with the lasso tight around my waist. Sasha started to giggle at my predicament.

Turning to face my captor, I said, "That was not fair." I stuck my tongue out at him as he jumped down from his horse.

As he approached, he pulled me in with the rope. "All's fair in love and war, Darlin'." When he came to the end of the rope he pulled me into his hard body and grinned at me. "Come riding with me, tonight?" I was trying to put some space between us because I could feel the heat from my blush starting on my face. However, he had a firm grip on me and I could not wriggle free. "You're cute when you blush," he teased.

"I don't think so, Cowboy. I haven't ridden for years. I don't think the horse would appreciate it," I said, smiling at him.

"Don't give me that. There is always time to relearn if ya forgot how to ride." He placed his hand on my neck and moved in closer to me. Our mouths were inches from each other. "Say ya will come riding with me and I'll let ya go."

Furiously blushing I nodded in agreement. "All right, but if I fall on my arse, I'm blaming you." He turned me around so he could untie the rope from around my waist. When I was free he swatted me on the rear end before walking away.

"And a nice arse it is too," he said, mimicking my accent. Whistling, he walked back to Sasha who was laughing at his antics.

**

I was sitting on my bed trying to decide what top to wear for our moonlight ride. It was going to be a cold tonight so I decided on a pair of jeans and a fur-lined jacket. However, I didn't know whether to wear a vest top or a ribbed top. Decisions, decisions. I never had this problem before. While I was debating my choices, Constance came in with some cowboy boots and a hat for me.

"Don't know what to wear?" she asked as she put the hat on the end table bed and the boots on the floor by it.

"Not a clue. I don't know why I agreed to it. I haven't been on a moonlit ride for years," I said, tapping my finger against my chin. I contemplated the pros and cons of both tops,

"May I make a suggestion?" she asked, heading toward the closet full of my mother's old shirts.

"Suggest away, Constance. I could use all the help I can get."

"Put the vest on but wear this over the top." Turning to me she handed me a stunning black shirt with a fancy trim on the arms.

"I can't wear that Constance. It's a moonlight ride not a rodeo," I remarked as she placed it on the bed next to the vest.

"Trust me, wear it. It'll look good on you as well as keep you warm. It is also quite comfortable and soft."

Without another word, she left the room. I picked up the velvet shirt and studied it. "Oh, well, what do I have to lose?"

**

To say I was nervous would be an understatement. As Blake would say, I was more nervous than a rabbit in a trap. I waited outside the barn doors for Blake to come out with the horses. He had asked me to grab the picnic basket and blanket that he had left on the table before coming out to the barn. So here I was holding a basket full of food waiting for the man himself.

"Here ya go Darlin'," he said as he walked out of the barn with Bertha and a white horse all ready saddled up. "Ready to go?" he asked placing a Stetson on my head. He was thoughtful enough to have a step stool ready for me so I could climb up easier as he held the white horse. The horse was well trained and posted absolutely still as I climbed into the saddle. He then secured the picnic basket and blanket to the back of his horse's saddle along with his guitar.

"So where are we going?" I asked as he spurred his horse to get her moving,

"I was thinking the overlook by Briar Ridge. We haven't been there since we were kids." Smiling at the memory, I thought back to the last time we were there.

"I don't want Marylou, Colleen, or Suzy. When I'm older I'm goin' t' marry ya, LJ ," Blake's younger voice said as he followed me toward the

watering hole. We are having one final swim before I have to head home to start my new job in the UK.

"Blake, honey, I'm three years older than you. You need someone your own age." Pulling to a stop so I could see the sun rising in the sky and reflecting on the water. I took a deep breath through my nose and exhaled through my mouth. I knew kids get crushes, but this was ridiculous. He was like my little brother.

"Pops says age is only a number. He loves my Mama and he is ten years older than her." Stamping his foot he moved toward the swimming hole to dip his foot in the water.

"That may be so, Blake but they are adults. When you are our age three years is a big gap." I crept up behind him and I pushed him in the water. He landed on his backside in the freezing lake. Glaring at me he slammed his hat into the water.

"LJ, that wasn't fair!" he yelled, sticking his lip out in a pout, "At least you could have waited until I had my clothes off." Smiling, I go to help him up, but he splashed water at me.

"Fine, be like that, you little shit. I was just trying to be nice." Taking off my shirt, I wrung out the excess water before stripping down to

my bathing suit. Jumping in the water, I swam toward the middle of the lake.

"LJ, Mama says not to go too far out into the lake. You might get your ya foot caught on the plants," he said, standing up to watch me as I swam further from the bank.

"Oh pish posh!" I exclaimed. "I've been swimming in this lake since before you were even born." Taking one last look at him I dove below the water and touched my feet to the bottom. I was about to swim back up when to my horror, I realized my foot was tangled on something. Someone had carelessly discarded a length of rope in the lake. I tried to free myself by tugging on my foot, but the rope only got tighter as I struggled. I didn't know how long I had been fighting to free my self, but it seemed like an eternity. My lungs were on fire by now and just as I was about to black out from the lack of oxygen I felt a hand grab my foot. Someone was sawing at the rope with a penknife. The moment I was freed I pushed myself back up to the surface. Exhausted and frightened from the near death experience, I felt Blake pulling me back to bank.

"See, I told ya not to go too deep." Once we got to the bank, I crawled on my hands and knees until I could feel dry land. Blake was

rubbing my back. "I'll never leave ya, LJ, ya can count on me." Smiling, I looked at Blake before lying on the ground to catch my breath.

"Thanks."

"Yeah, you made your point about not swimming too far in the lake." I stole a glance at Blake and I could see he had a smile on his face as he remembered the same memory.

"Do ya remember what I told ya that day?" I nodded my head and pressed the horse to go faster. I could see the lookout up ahead and I really didn't want to talk about what he said that day, "I told ya I would marry ya someday LJ ," Blake yelled as he caught up to me. He pulled on the reins to slow me down. Taking hold of my hand he kissed the knuckles. "I promise ya one day ya will realize that there is more to life than what y'all have had. Making that promise was a childhood crush, but I meant it. And I will mean it 'til my last breath. I'm going to marry ya one day." He leaned over his horse and before I knew it he was kissing me full on the mouth. I found myself losing all self control. My hands found themselves crawling up his body until they were entwined around his neck. Yes, I kissed him back. I couldn't help myself. "And I always keep my promises," he stated as he pulled away, leaving my mouth agape. He rode off ahead, leaving me to stare in shock at his retreating back.

Chapter 13

"My favourite was always the story about Orion the hunter," I said, using a stick to draw the constellation in the bare earth in front of us. "His life was so tragic because he angered the Earth Goddess, Gaia. Poor Artemis. She never knew how jealous her brother Apollo was. Imagine that being the reason your best friend died. I don't think I could have lived with myself if it had been me." I leaned back on my hands and looked at all the constellations that were etched in the black skies. Thing about being out here, there were no lights from the city to dim the stars. Laying back down, I took a deep breath of the cold night air.

"Personally, Darlin', I never did like the stories of the stars. They were always so tragic. And sad. I'd rather imagine that all the stars are fallen heroes, immortalized for all eternity," Blake said. We were laying on the cool ground with the top of our heads touching.

"Do you remember the stories I told you when we were kids about what shooting stars were." Sitting up again, I rotated my shoulders to get circulation back in them. I found that as I got older the more aches and pains I had. A strong pair of hands started to massage the knots in my shoulder.

"Yes, and ya terrified me with the story of Chicken Little. I ran home crying to my Mama because I was so scared that the sky was falling." He placed his chin on my shoulder and put his face close to mine. "But when Mama told me about wishing on a shooting star, I only ever had one wish..." He looked at me before turning away, "...for my girl to come home." I reached out to play with his hair and smiled at him.

"You're such a doofus!" Laughing, I reached for his guitar case and opened it. "So when are you going to show me how well you play this thing?" He took the guitar out of the case and sat on the bank. I laid back down and stared at the stars above us.

"Here is the one I wrote a long time ago called "Love Ain't easy." Strumming his fingers against the strings I felt my mind begin to wander as the lyrics fill my heart with awe. Not only could he sing and play, but he wrote his own lyrics and music too.

"I met her on the highway ridin' shotgun.

I can still recall that purple dress she wore.

She was sobbin' at the toll booth by the off-ramp,

and I knew no guy would ever love her more.

She asked me if I'd stay with her forever.

She said to me there was no other guy.

But who'd have thought she'd run off with my best friend.

You'd think at least that she'd have said goodbye."

"That's really good Blake. So very tragic," I remarked as he strummed the last chord. He just smiled and shrugged his shoulders.

"Well, when in Texas..." he replied before going back to strumming his guitar. Looking at him in the silvery moonlight, I could see why the women seemed to flock around him. He continued to play and the shadows cast his face into darkness, giving him a mysterious air about him, His face relaxed as he got sucked back into the music coming out of his guitar.

"I met her outside Fresno in September.

I can still recall that little hat she wore.

She was crawlin' through the prairie in the twilight,

and I knew that she was rotten to the core."

"Why are country songs so tragic; can't you come up with happier lyrics?" I asked as I crawled next to him. I instructed him to play C, D, Am and F chords over and over.

Riding horseback along the fields
You're so close but still a world away
Warm brown eyes and sparkling smile
You'd be so perfect with me but you just can't see

All my dreams come true
My life has been such a whirlwind since I saw you
Lost in the moment
I'm crazy for you

Forever and a day
Cause I've done everything I know
Too shy for them to notice
Can't you feel the weight of my stare

All my dreams come true
My life has been such a whirlwind since I saw you

Lost in the moment
I'm crazy for you

He looked at me and laughed before setting his guitar aside and pulling me into his arms.

"That is just as bad as having a broken heart," he said, grinning.

"Hey, at least she didn't run off with your best friend... or his tractor." Pulling his arms tighter around me, I looked up at the skies and saw a shooting star. "Look!" I said, pointing.

"Make a wish Darlin'," he said. However, before I could form a sentence, he leaned around and kissed me on the cheek.

I turned around to look at him and smirked. "I thought I was supposed to make a wish?"

"Sorry, but you hesitated," he said with a shrug. I opened my mouth to protest when suddenly and without warning he pulled me in to him and pressed his lips to mine. His mouth and tongue begged me to open up to him. Letting myself lean forward, I eagerly opened up as our lips started a seductive dance with each other. Getting my sense back before it went too far, I pulled away and raised my hand to my lips. I stared at him in bewilderment.

"Blake, um...I can't. I'm sorry but I can't do this." Standing up, I walked toward the horse and prepare to climb into the saddle.

"LJ, come on, you know I've been in love with ya since we were kids. I told ya then that I was going to marry ya. Why can't you just see that and love me back?" Blake asked, grabbing my arm and turning me around to face him.

"Blake, be real. Look at me I'm a thirty six year old, overweight woman whose husband was cheating on her. You can have your pick of women, why me? What on Earth do you see in me?" I asked, Putting hands on my hips in annoyance I waited for an answer, He wasn't making this easy that's for sure.

"I don't want to speak ill of the dead, but..."

"Then don't..." I said, not wanting to hear it. I knew where this was going.

But he continued, "Carl was an idiot and a damn fool. He had a good thing and he threw it all away. He never deserved you or your love. You are beautiful, caring and an awesome mother to Sasha." Cupping my face in his calloused hands, I could feel bolts of electricity flow from the contact. When he started to smooth his fingers just under my hairline I swear I turned to goo.

"Blake, don't. I can't do this." I tried to turn away, but he held me tight and leaned toward me. "Blake, what are you doing?" Swiftly, he placed his soft lips against mine.

"I love you LJ, I always have." He tried to kiss again, I pulled away.

"No Blake! No! I made a promise and I can't go back on it." Turning away from him, I prepared myself to jump back into the saddle. I looked back at him one last time and saw the pain in his eyes. "I'm sorry."

"LJ, ya can't keep running away from what we have here!" he implored making his way to his horse as I tried to turn my steed around. I was determined to head back to the ranch. I didn't want to have this conversation. Unexpectedly, he grabbed my shoulder, causing me to shrink back from him. Seeing this, he backed down, calming his tone. "You've had a tough time of it, I get it," he said gently. "But you need to listen to me. Your husband was a jack ass who didn't know what a good thing he had." His cheeks burned red. I didn't know if it was because he was angry at me or at Carl. Perhaps he was angry at the world in general. "He cheated on ya because he knew that ya were too good for him. Yet he kept you under his thumb because that is the kind of ass he was. I don't understand why don't ya let yourself be happy?"

Turning to face him with tears of anger pouring from my eyes, I shouted, "You don't get it, do you, Blake? He was my whole world! He didn't leave me for another woman! He died and I heard him die! It was all my fault. I wasn't the wife he deserved. I wasn't with him when he died! I should have been with him."

"My, God, LJ, how can you even think it was your fault?"

With a frustrated groan, I snatched the reins from his hand and prepared to ride away. I no longer wanted to deal with the subject. "Find yourself a nice, young, cowgirl and settle down. I'm broken."

"I refuse to believe that."

"Listen, I made a promise. I promised him that if anything ever happened to him I would never look at another man. It was the last promise I made and I will keep it."

He leaned close enough that I could see the hurt in his eyes. "He was a selfish man who should never have made you make that promise. I'd bet if the roles were reversed, he'd break that promise in a microsecond. The bastard cheated on ya and yet ya pine after him like a school girl. You should be thinking about yourself not about a promise he forced on you. I would wager that he forced a lot of demands on you..." Suddenly I heard a sharp crack sound. I hadn't realized that I just slapped my best friend across his face. He stepped back looking like a beat puppy. He slowly rubbed his reddening cheek. To my surprise he just smiled at me. "Now, there's the little spitfire I remember." Stepping back, he let me climb back into the saddle. "Dammit, LJ. If ya won't fight for us then I guess I will have to for the both of us.." He turned and went back to his own horse. Sobbing, I dug my heels into my horse and rode away from him. I needed my space. Space from him and space from my own feelings about my life.

Chapter 14

Blake had been avoiding me since the night of our fight. It seemed that every time I would enter a room he was in, he would leave without saying a word. Knowing he was upset and it was all my fault didn't give me any comfort. My heart felt like it was broken in two. He was avoiding me and I never wanted that to happen. It was all my fault. I pushed him away. I destroyed the only man who had my back through both good and bad times.

As the days started to heat up, I often found myself riding my horse in the fields. I rode to the far-reaching boundaries of the ranch just to get away. Sometimes Sasha would come with me and other days she would hang around the ranch and spend time with our Uncle and Blake. She seemed to sense something was wrong, but never said a thing. That left me to contemplate my own thoughts as I tried to escape the hurt I have caused him. Truth be told, my feelings for Blake continued to grow every day but, I kept hearing Carl's voice in my head. He constantly told me that I had made a promised never to look at another man. It left a hollow feeling in my chest and I knew that I couldn't break that promise. A promise I made when I was still pregnant with Sasha....

Lying on the blanket in the picturesque hills of the Brecon Beacons, we watched the fireworks from the surrounding towns light up the sky,

"I don't understand why you want to go back to the ranch? Go to America, for God's sake," he said as the sky lit up with a multitude of rockets, "This is your home. I have my job and you have yours. Why would you throw it all away?" Looking at my husband I rubbed my hand across the stubble on his face.

I placed my hand on my growing belly. The baby seemed to be doing restless somersaults within my womb. "Why shouldn't we go back? We have no family here, but we have family in Texas." Taking his hand in mine, I placed it on my stomach and let him feel the baby kicking up a storm.

"We have a life here babe, why can't you see that? I said I would take care of you both, but there is no guarantee I can get a job over there. And I don't see myself working on a ranch. Mucking out shit from horse stalls and mending fences for the rest of my life just isn't my dream job."

Looking him squarely in the eye I huff ever so slightly. "Carl, you could get a job in Austin. It is only 30 minutes from the ranch. With your skills in IT, you would be able to walk into any job." Arguing with him never helped ,but I was damned if I was going to back down from him.

"That is beside the point, LJ. I've worked hard to get where I am, I can't just throw that away on a whim."

Standing up, I took a few steps away before crossing my arms over my chest. "It is not a whim. Maybe I should just go on my own if that is how you feel?" He stood up and walked over to me. Placing his hands on my shoulders, I feel him massaging them as he planted soft kisses on my neck.

"That is not what I meant baby and you know it. Just let me think on it. If it is possible then we will go, but I don't want to make any rash decisions." Turning me around to face him he kissed me tenderly on the lips. "I can't live without you baby. Please don't leave me. We agreed to be married for all eternity." Taking me in his arms he started to rock me like a baby. "I couldn't bear if you left me. You need to promise me one thing...." I feel my body start to melt into his embrace. I hated arguing with him.

"Anything?" I said wanting nothing more than to see him happy.

"Promise me that if anything happens to me you will not look at another man. I couldn't bear the thought of someone else making love to you or raising our child. You are mine, body and soul."

Looking into his eyes, tears slowly fell down my face. "I promise."

**

So now here I was breaking the one promise I did intend to keep to my husband. I did not know what to do? I realized that I had been riding aimlessly and ended up close to the lake where I had nearly drowned so many years ago. I looked up at the clear sky and decided to take a dip in the cool water to clear my mind. The lake was the only place where I felt happy and was able to forget about all that had happened in the last month. Slipping my clothes off, I stepped into the cool water to try and figure out how I was going to solve this dilemma I now faced.

**

Blake picked himself up from the ground and limped over to Bertha who decided to throw him from the saddle again. He was trying to practice his rodeo routine, but Bertha was not having any it. His horse could sense his agitation and that meant she was going to do what she wanted. Sort of like LJ. LJ had run off again and Blake couldn't concentrate because she was constantly on his mind. Every morning she would leave at the crack of dawn and not return until well into the night. He had no idea where she went for so many hours but he noticed that she had stopped eating. He could see the toll that starving herself was taking on her body, but he didn't know how to help her.

"Blake, have you seen my Mama?" Sasha asked from the barn door where she was brushing Meadow's mane.

"I don't know sweetheart. She went off early this morning." Picking up his hat from the ground, he slapped the dust off.

"Is Mama okay? I heard her crying again last night."

Taking a step toward the little girl, he squatted down so he could look her in the eyes. "What ya mean she has been crying again?" he asked, sitting on the bale of hay by the door. Sasha put the brush in the bucket by her feet as she sat next to him. "The other night I woke up when I heard Mama screaming. I think she was having another bad dream. I went into her room and found her clutching at the sheet crying out Daddy's name." Laying her hand on Blake's, she sniffed as tears started to roll down her face, "I know Mama misses Daddy. I do too. But, I don't like hearing her scream in her sleep."

Wanting to comfort the little girl he placed an arm around her shoulders to pulled her in for a tight hug. "Its all right, sweetheart, your Mama is just grieving. She will never get over your Daddy." Realising that tears are starting to escape his eyes he quickly wiped them away, but Sasha noticed.

"Are you grieving too, Blake?" she asked, not understanding why her Mama's friend was crying.

"Kinda, sweetheart, but for different reasons than your Mama."

Looking up at him, she appeared confused. "Who have you lost, Blake?" she asked, laying a comforting hand on his arm.

"I've lost my best friend, sweetheart," he replied, gathering her in his arms.

The young girl was more astute than he realized. "Do you love my Mama? Is she why you are upset?" she asked as she climbed up on the hay bale to wrap her arms around his shoulders in a comforting gesture. She gave him a little kiss on the cheek.

"You're too young to understand this, sweetheart."

"I'm 12, not 4. If you love my Mama you need to tell her. The only time I see her happy is when she is with you. I don't want to see her cry anymore. I love my Daddy and I know Mama does too, but he isn't here anymore. I just want her to stop crying at night," she said with the innocence of a child. "If you could help my Mama so she didn't cry anymore I would be so happy."

"Do ya think I should go and find her?" he asked.

She looked up at him with happiness and nodded. "Yes, you need to find my Mama so she will smile again." He gave Sasha a kiss on the head before he stood up. He would have to lay it all on the table and put the ball in her court. It would be up to her to come to him. However he would have to find her first. It dawned on him where the only place where she would go to think about her problems was the same place she used to go as a kid. It was also the place where he would go every year when she failed to come back to visit. The lake.

**

After swimming a few hours, my legs started to grow tired so I just floated on my back to recover. I let the water take my weight and I realised that I couldn't remember the last time I had actually had something more substantial than a piece of toast to eat. I was struggling to swim back to the bank. I didn't have any energy left to swim. I lowered my legs and tread the water for a time. The sun was starting to go down and the air bounced across the still water. This started to bring a chill and the goose bumps that came with it.

Shivering with cold and panic, I spotted a rock formation coming out of the water and, with every ounce of energy I could muster, I tried to swim to the rock. However, my tired body started to seize up as the cold water affected my weary bones and muscles. Panic started to set in when I realized that there was no way to get to dry land. Cold water flowed over my head I resigned myself to my fate, waiting for the inevitable. I had given up on life. I prayed for forgiveness and last thoughts would be for my daughter, my deceased husband and the cowboy I was leaving behind. They would be the ones to suffer because I didn't have the words or the strength to tell him that I was in love with him. With one last push, I broke the surface to take what might have been my last breath before the water pulled me back down again. I didn't hear the voice screaming my name....

Chapter 15

As he rode toward the lake he could see the white horse that LJ had taken on her ride. The horse was in noticeable distress, pacing and whinny along the bank. Jumping down from his horse, he ran down the bank where he spotted LJ's clothes on the rocks. Shielding his eyes from the setting sun, he cupped his hands around his mouth and shouted across the lake.

"LJ! LJ! Where are ya?" he shouted, then waited to see if he could hear an answering shout or splash of water but the lake remained eerily quiet. Suddenly both of the horses lifted their heads and looked across the lake where there was a sudden splash of water. He looked in the same direction and saw LJ come up gasping for air before the lake water pulled her back down.

"LJ!" he yelled, pulling off his boots and jumping into the icy water. Pushing his body to the limit he swam to the area where he last saw the splash of water. Taking a deep breath he dove into the murky depths. He couldn't see anything under the water so he had to resort to blind searching with his hands. Feeling around he grabbed what felt like a frozen arm. He pulled the still body toward him and swam to the surface. He used a rescue swimming technique with an inverted breaststroke while keeping LJ's head above water to make his way back to the bank. The horses were stomping their feet in agitation. "Hold on Darlin'...don't leave me," he said, knowing that every second counted, he pushed himself past the tiredness and cold to get LJ to dry land.

Finally, after what seemed like an eternity of swimming he dragged her limp body up onto the bank. Laying her flat on her back, he shook her shoulders while calling out her name, "LJ, can ya hear me, honey?" He got no response and he lifted her chin, placing his ear to her mouth to see if she was breathing. She was turning blue and not breathing. He felt for a pulse with one hand and dialled 911 with the other. Finding no pulse, he started CPR. When the dispatcher answered, he placed the phone on speaker, giving them a location and informing them that he had started CPR. As each minute passed he could feel his heart breaking. If he failed her, he didn't know what he would do. Just the thought of never seeing her smile again made him continue the chest compressions for what seemed like forever. In actuality it was only a few minutes. He looked up when he heard the sound of a medical helicopter landing on a clearing. A sudden coughing up of water brought his attention back to LJ. She was breathing again, but retching up the dirty lake water. "It's okay, just cough it up." He turned her on her side in the recovery position so the water she was coughing up wouldn't go back into her lungs. He whipped off his jacket and covered her to keep her warm as the medics arrived with a stretcher.

**

A consistent beeping pulled me from my dark slumber. My eyes were blurry but I seemed to be in a white room. *Is this heaven,* I wondered. No, this isn't heaven. I started to panic when I realized that something was down my throat. A vision in pink entered my vision and placed a hand on my shoulder.

"Shh, sweetie, be still. You are intubated. Relax and I will remove the endotracheal tube. It's going to feel like you are gagging, but its only for a moment, Okay?"

I nodded my head at the lady whose name tag reads Nurse Rickter. She was gentle but mercifully quick to remove the tube from my throat. I gagged and coughed once I was free to breath on my own.

"You might have a sore throat for a few days. You gave us quite a scare, young lady." Her facial features finally came into focus. I could see wrinkles on tanned skin and wisps of white hair escaping the tight bun at the nape of her neck.

"Where..." Swallowing, I tried again to speak. "Where am I?"

Smiling, the nurse pulled the blanket up to my chin. "You at Austin Lakes hospital, sweetie. They brought you in on the medical helicopter a couple of days ago."

"Oh, yeah, I remember now. I was swimming...."

"Shh, it's all over now. You will be just fine. Hey, there is someone outside in the waiting room. He has not left your side since you came in. We tried to get him to go home, but he refused to move until you woke up. Should I send him in?" Not waiting for my answer, she left the room to fetch whoever it was who was waiting for me. A few minutes later I looked up to see Blake standing in the doorway. He had a couple of days worth of stubble on his face which made him look extremely sexy. As he was walking toward the bed I could feel my heart skip a beat. Smiling, he leaned over and placed a chaste kiss on my forehead before sitting beside the bed.

Taking my hand in his, he said, "Ya had me worried, Darlin'," he said, playing with my hair. "I didn't think I would get ya breathing at the lake." Studying him, I could see the dark bags under his red-rimmed eyes and his face seemed to have aged dramatically making him appear older than his thirty three years.

I tried to speak, but my throat felt like it was on fire. It took a few minutes for me to find my voice. "I'm sorry I worried you," I said with a hoarse voice as he continued to stroke my hair. "How did you find me?" I took hold of his hand because his playing with my hair was very distracting.

"I had a talk with Sasha; she said y'all had been screaming in your sleep again at night. So I went to look for you. Why didn't ya tell me ya weren't sleeping properly again, Darlin'? And don't think I haven't noticed ya haven't been eating properly either!" He looked at me with a disapproving look.

"I'm sorry. It's just my that head has been all over the place lately." Looking away, I tried to focus on the picture of the poppies on the opposite wall.

"Hey..." he said, using his finger to guide my eyes back to his. "Why did ya turn away?" Shrugging my shoulders I looked down. Truth be told I felt embarrassed that I put him through all that worry. I thought I was doing a pretty good job of hiding everything. But Sasha and Blake had noticed the changes in my behaviour.

"Look, LJ, I need to tell ya something. Seeing ya laying and there not breathing, I thought my heart was going stop beating along with yours..." Looking into his eyes, I waited for him to carry on. "LJ ...ya have to know by now that I lo..." He never got to finish his sentence.

"Mama!" Sasha shouted, bounding into the room and jumping on my bed. "Mama are you okay?" she asked, wrapping her arms around my neck. She looked almost as worried as Blake. It must have taken all of Constance and Uncle Pete's power to keep her at home.

"I'm all right, little Dove, but I can't breath...ease up on the hug, sweetie." I gave her a quick hug and a kiss on the cheek before letting her go. Uncle Pete and Constance were in the doorway with smiles on their faces. They gave me a wave as they let me have time with my daughter. The nurse entered the room behind them.

"Okay, everyone, including you, out!" she said, pointedly looking at Blake, "LJ needs her rest. The doctor said he will discharge her tomorrow if she is rested enough. You all need to all go home and get some sleep." She rested a hand on my shoulder before shooing my family out the door.

"Give me a minute," Blake said. The nurse nodded but raised one finger to signify one minute more.

"Blake...you need to go home and rest. You look like shit." Taking his hand in mine I rubbed my fingers across his knuckles.

"Thanks, so do you."

"And thank you," I laughed, but instantly regretted it. "Ow."

"Before I go I wanted to do this." He suddenly pressed his lips to mine then just a quickly pulled away. "Don't you ever scare me like that again, y'hear?." he said in a stern tone as he stroked my face. "I'll pick ya up tomorrow, but then I'll be leaving the ranch for a while."

"What? Why?"

"The Austin Rodeo is starting in a couple of days. Being that I am their reigning champion, I need to be there."

I nodded my head, but inside I'm frozen, I didn't realize the rodeo was happening so soon. Grinning he gave me one more light kiss before leaving the room. I could hear Sasha talking to him as they walked down the hall away from my room.

Chapter 16

Still in the hospital room, I paced the floor while waiting for my
discharge. Blake had phoned the hospital to tell them he was running late.
One of the fences had fallen so he and Uncle Pete were trying to find all the
cattle that had escaped. That was four hours ago and I was starting to get
antsy. I picked up a trashy magazine that one of the night nurses had given
me to occupy my mind. I sat on the bed and opened the magazine. Maybe
reading about the latest celebrity scandal would take my mind off the
boredom while I sat there patiently for my cowboy to arrive.

**

It was starting to get dark by the time Pete and he had found all the
cattle. It looked like someone had cut through the fence. The livestock was
wandering the neighbouring fields and it took hours to get them all back.
Knowing he still needed to pick up LJ from the hospital, he jumped into his
rusted blue pinto truck for the 45-minute drive to the hospital. He didn't
think she could last one more night in that place. She was a typical
homebody and needed to be with her family, not surrounded by strangers.
Just as he was turning in the direction of the hospital, his phone rang
startling him with the sudden loudness that disrupted his quiet solitude.

"Howdy," he said, answering the phone. He turned high beams in order to penetrate the dark night.

"Blake. Finally. I've been trying to get a hold of you for hours!" The voice of his rodeo partner and friend Randy McCall came from the blue-tooth speaker of his truck.

"Randy. Someone cut the fence at Coyote Lodge; I've been rounding up cows all day." Blake could hear his friend talking to someone else in the background.

"Well I'm sorry ta hear that. A few of the cattle farmers in your area have been talking about the same thing happening at their homesteads." he stated. There was a lot of background noise on the call and it was hard to hear him.

"How many 'ave said their fences were cut?" he asked, turning into the hospital grounds.

"Ten Beeves farmers in your area," Randy replied before telling someone away from the phone that he would be there in a minute. Pulling to a stop in an empty space he picked up his phone from the holder and placed it to his ear.

"Okay, I'll let Pete know. I got to gitty-up and pick up my gal from the hospital." Blake said as he walked toward the hospital entrance.

"You got a gal? You're dirty ole dog. What's her name? Where did you meet?" Laughing, Blake entered the hospital and made his way to LJ's room,

"Y'all remember LJ? Well she's back," he said as he pushed his way through the ward door.

"That sweet little thing you had a crush on as a kid? When did she roll back into town?" Randy asked.

"A couple of months ago. Her husband died in a car crash and she finally came back home."

"Well damn, partner, you sure you wanna come to the rodeo?" Blake made his way to LJ's room and spotted her sitting on the bed reading a trashy magazine.

"Of course. The rodeo needs its reignin' bronco champ." LJ saw Blake walking into the room and smiled at him. "I got to go. See ya tomorrow afternoon, Randy." He quickly disconnected the phone just in time to catch LJ as she ran to him for a hug.

**

I heard a voice in the corridor outside my room and looked up to see Blake talking on his phone. The moment he hung up I ran to him and gave him a massive hug, "You're late!" Hugging him tight, I didn't want to let him go. He was grinning at me. "What?"

"I told ya I would pick ya up, didn't I?" he said in his sexy Texas accent. "I just didn't know I'd be this late." He picked up my bag of belongings from the bed. "Let's get you home to rest."

"If I rest any more, I'll go stark raving mad."

"You mean ya aren't already?'

I gave him a playful punch in the arm. Grinning he led me out of the room by the elbow.

**

Once I got home I was ready for my bed. Hospitals did not have the most comfortable beds. Since Blake was traveling to the rodeo tomorrow, I wanted to spend more time with him. While my mind was conflicted about my feelings for Blake, my heart was another matter entirely. It would take time for my mind to catch up with my heart. I still doubted that I was doing the right thing. It weighed heavily on my conscience. It was like an internal battle within my soul.

Do I break the promise I made to Carl and find happiness again or do I keep the promise and live an unfulfilled life? It sounded like an easy choice, but in reality it was the hardest thing I ever had to face. What Blake had said still echoed in my mind. He said that Carl was a selfish bastard for making me promise something like that. Nonetheless, it was a promise made out of love and commitment. The saying of what the heart wants the heart gets is true, however, with my mind a whirlwind of doubt and self-loathing my heart's desire was slowly fading into the abyss.

Sitting on the back porch, I waited until Blake came out to join me. He had two soda bottles in his hand. After giving me one, he sat down next to me.

Taking a sip, he asked, "Are you goin' to be okay while I'm gone?"

I want to say no, but I know the rodeo was his dream ever since he was a child. "I'll be fine Blake. You've been talking about the rodeo for as long as I can remember. What kind of person would I be if I got in the way of your dream?" Placing a friendly arm around my shoulders he gave me a gentle squeeze.

"You can come with me if you want. I certainly won't mind."

Letting myself rest in his arms, I played with the bottle in my hand before answering him. "I wish I could. But I've not been to a rodeo in a long time and Uncle Pete needs at least one of us here to help." Smiling at him I took hold of his hand and give it a gentle squeeze. "Although it is tempting." Settling into the embrace we both watched the fireflies dance across the pastures. They were like little twinkling lights floating in the breeze.

"You need ta promise me one thing," Blake said, finishing up the soda. I looked at him in confusion.

"What?"

"Stay away from the lake. If something happens I won't be there to pull you out." Turning, so I'm kneeling on the bench to face him I take his face in my hands.

"I promise. But you promise me one thing too? Be careful, anything can happen when you are on that bucking bronco."

He placed his hand on mine and I licked my lips. The tension was rising in anticipation of a kiss, but before I could close the gap between us, the door swung open and my Uncle shadowed the light.

"Oh sorry," Uncle Pete said. "I didn't realize you two were still out here." He quickly went back in the house, closing the door behind him.

Laughing at his antics, I looked at Blake. I could see the corners of his mouth tilting up into a smile.

"His timing sucks," Blake said.

"I think that is what is called a cock block."

"Nah," he said, leaning forward to catch my mouth in a sweet kiss before he pulled me onto his lap. The kiss deepened and I was breathing heavy. I had to pull back to catch my breath.

Looking him in the eyes, I said, "Blake, I don't know if we are doing the right thing here."

"Nonsense,"

"I mean...." Holding his face in my hands I noticed his perfect cheekbones. I couldn't help but to trace them with my fingertips. Meanwhile there was a raging inferno boiling in the pit of my stomach.

"What's wrong about it Darlin'? I know you can feel what I'm feelin'. There is nothin' wrong with having those feelings' LJ."

"I know, but I'm scared to feel like this again." Kissing the palm of his hand I decided there and then that I couldn't let my fear take over my life. "But what if we do this and it ruins our friendship? I don't want to ruin one of the two good things I still have in my life." I felt tears start to run down my face and I lowered my eyes so he could not see the fear in the depths.

"LJ, don't ever hide what you're feelin' with me." Using his hand, he lifted up my face to so I could look him square in his eyes. "We have been friends for a long time. If we try this and it doesn't work then we will still be friends. But I don't want to live my life knowin' that we didn't even try." I lowered my lips to his and let the kiss deepen to show the multitude of my feelings in that one simple touch and caress. Placing my forehead against his, I noticed both of us were now breathing heavy. It was like there was not enough air around to give us the oxygen we needed to keep on living. He used my hair as a handle to pull my face up gently so I could look into his eyes. "If I never get a chance ta having anything else with you, I will cherish that kiss. It means you do feel something for me too."

"Oh, course I do, Blake." Smiling, he placed his hands behind my neck and pulled me in for another scorching kiss.

**

Up in my room, the kiss deepened as Blake started kneading his fists into my back while the heat grew between us. Anticipation twirled around my body as Blake nuzzled my neck, kissing and nibbling, making my breath catch in my throat and my skin to flush.

"Darlin' if you don't want to go too fast we won't," he said as he started to undo the buttons of my shirt. Chills erupted on my skin as the cool night air brushed across me. Blake slowly lowered my shirt and it landed on the floor behind me. Feeling self-conscious, I tried to hide my bra by crossing my arms over my chest, but Blake gently pulled them back down to my sides, "Don't ever think you need ta hide from me." He lowered the straps of my bra with his fingertips before reaching round to unclasp the back. It hung briefly beneath my breasts before it too ended up with my shirt. Tracing his fingertips from my neck down to my chest he swirled his fingers to the centre of the aching mounds. Unbuttoning my jeans, he lowered them to the floor. Feeling slightly self conscious and uncomfortable I shifted my weight. Seeing this he stood up and wrapped an arm around my waist, pulling me in to a kiss. My hands were shaking as I slowly unbuttoned his shirt. Gently I traced my fingers along his well defined body and the strawberry colored birthmark which was just below his belly button. The birthmark disappeared into the trail of hair that lead into his jeans. Wanting to see more of him I kissed his neck before taking hold of the buttons on his pants to pull them apart. Eventually he was just standing there in his boxers.

"We can stop you know." he said as he lowered me onto the bed. Shaking my head, I gave him a kiss before pulling away.

"I ca..can't"

"It's all right. Come on Darlin' lets get some sleep?"

Chapter 17

In the morning while cradled in Blake's arms I felt a sense of peace. Even though we didn't go any further than the kissing last night it was comforting just having someone sleep next to me. Holding me in his arms helped chased away the nightmares that had been plaguing me for the last two months. Looking at him sleeping, I was reminded our age difference. I mean he was younger than me. Examining the features in his face, I noticed that the harsh lines melted away as he rested in peaceable slumber. The was the young men I once knew. Tracing my fingertip along his lip, I smiled as the corners of his mouth turned up just for me. It made my heart swell with love, but there was also a slither of doubt in my mind.

What the hell was I doing? Could I really let myself fall for my best friend in this way when my husband was barely two months in the ground? I think I had already taken a step into the chasm that would cause me to fall into its fiery depths. As I contemplated my internal dilemma his eyes opened and he looked at me.

"Mornin' Darlin'," he cooed, in reply I laid my head down on his chest. I could hear his heartbeat. He smiled and wrapped his arms around me, holding me tight. "Mmm, what' time is it?" he asked but he did not attempted to reach for his phone on the bedside table.

"It's still early. I don't think anyone else is awake yet apart from Uncle Pete." Reaching across him I picked up his phone and saw that it was 6 am in the morning. As I showed him the time, he cussed and jumped out of bed.

"Damn why didn't Pete call me! I said I'd help out with milkin' the cows before I left for the rodeo." Smiling I watched as he pulled on his jeans and shirt. When he turned to face me I couldn't help but blush at the sight of his well-defined body before the shirt covered him.

"Don't leave without saying goodbye. okay?" He leaned over and gave me a kiss. I grabbed his shirt and pulled him in closer before reluctantly releasing him.

**

Pulling on his boots he ran down to the milking shed where Pete was about half-way through milking them. "Why didn't ya call me, Pete?" he asked, pulling up a stool to start milking the cow next to him.

"I did come to your room, but ya weren't there," Pete said, raising a bushy eyebrow, "Where did ya sleep last night?"

Rubbing the back of his neck as if he was thinking of what to say, he replied, "I stayed with LJ last night." Honesty was the best policy with Pete. The man had an uncanny ability to spot a lie a mile away.

"Don' you go hurtin' my niece, Blake. I love ya like a son, but she is my blood." Pete said, pulling himself up to his full height and squaring off at Blake. The older man was actually challenging him.

Holding his hand to his heart, Blake said. "I would never hurt her, Pete. I care about her too much to ever hurt her." The old man looked at the young cowboy. All he needed was a shotgun to complete the look.

"That is the problem, boy. You care about her a little too much. How you know ya aren't projecting your emotions onto her."

Blake stopped what he was doing and looked at the old Rancher. "How do ya mean?"

"Use your brain, Son. She was widowed just a little over two months ago. Not only that she found out he was cheating on her and was getting ready to leave her. She is in emotional turmoil."

Blake started to understand what Pete was saying, but he still thought what he was doing was the right thing for her. "Pete, I know that."

"Listen to me, boy. She's gone from being widowed from a man who said he didn't love her anymore to this young buck who has been around her most of her life—as her best friend...." Pete paused for a moment, patting the hindquarters of the cow he was milking. "You are someone she has trusted for years and declaring your feelings for her like you do, well, It's gonna be too much for her to handle. In her mind until she can love herself again, she can't love anyone else. Perhaps even, she doesn't feel worthy of their love." Pete placed a hand on Blake's shoulder, "I know ya care about her, son, but you need to let her mourn and figure out what she needs. You don't want to be rebound guy. Until she can figure out her feelings you shouldn't project your emotions onto her."

Blake stands there, thinking of what Pete had just said and then just walked toward the barn door. "I got to go."

"Where ya goin'?"

"I need to speak to LJ and leave." Turning around he walked back over to Pete and shook his hand. "I'll see ya in a couple of months." Exiting the barn, Blake made his way back to the house. He needed to tell LJ how he felt before he left for the rodeo.

**

Standing in the kitchen and washing up the breakfast dishes, I jumped when the door slammed behind me. Startled, I dropped one of the bowls on the floor and it smashed into a dozen pieces.

"Dammit." Gritting my teeth I squat down to pick up the broken pieces just as another pair of hands join me.

"Sorry," Blake said, bending down and picking up the pieces. "I didn't mean to scare ya."

I shrugged my shoulders and said, "You didn't. I was deep in thought is all." He dropped the broken pieces of the bowl in the trash. I noticed the frown on his face and asked, "Why are you so serious? Is everything okay?"

"I need to tell ya somethin'," he said, leading me to the dining room chair.

"Okay, you are scaring me. What is it, Blake?"

"LJ listen to me. I hav'ta tell you this. I'm in love with ya, but I need ya to take this time while I'm at the rodeo to figure out if ya really love me or if I'm just a rebound guy."

"Blake...." I started protest, but he placed his hand on my chin, running his thumb across my lips

"No, don't say anything yet. Jus' promise me that ya will take the time I'm away ta think abou' it."

"I promise."

He helped me out of the chair and pulled in to a scorching, knee-weakening kiss. "I'll see ya when I get back."

"Good luck."

Before walking out the door, he looked back at me one last time and winked. I waved and he vanished from sight. Sitting back down at the table, I ran my fingers along my lips where I could still feel Blake's kiss. I had a lot to think about.

Chapter 18

The day that he had left for the rodeo was the hardest thing he ever had to do. All he wanted to do was take her in his arms and not let her go. He wanted to shower her with kisses and show her how desirable she was to him. Nevertheless, the wise old rancher was correct. She was still mourning her husband even thought he treated her like dirt. She had to figure out for herself and when she was ready for them to take the next step or stay just as friends. He hoped that she would consider taking things further, but he didn't want to push her. He had a very persuasive personality and if his feelings clouded hers then he would never know if they could truly work or would just fizzle out. He loved her with a passion, but she needed to figure out if her feelings were real or a projection of his own.

**

Pulling the car into a parking lot at a local bar, Blake and Randy made their way into the packed room. It was full of cowboys and gals looking for a bit of release before the competition became too much for all of them to get along civilly once tempers flew.

"I'm glad you are back, Blake," Randy said to him as he ordered them a couple of beers. "I never get see you anymore." Taking a drink, he raised his glass to his friend.

"It had been a long time, but I'm here now," Blake said, watching the crowd start up an impromptu two step in the middle of the dance floor.

"So what have you been up to?" Randy asked, looking at the ladies out on the dance floor shaking their hips to the beat of the music. "Pete told me you spent time in the UK for a bit?"

"Yeah, I went to be with LJ. Her husband died in a car crash so she needed a friend to hold her hand." Randy looked at him with a knowing smile.

"LJ, huh? The girl you have been mooning over for longer than I have known you?" Seeing his friend's ashen face, Randy placed a reassuring hand on his shoulder. "Was it that bad?"

"No," he replied, taking a sip of his drink. "It was nice to spend some time with her and her daughter, Sasha. I told ya she came back to the ranch a couple of months ago."

"And?"

"Well we got closer and I told her how I felt about her," he said as he drained the beer from the bottom of the mug.

"So, how did it go? And why are you at the rodeo?" Randy asked him as he raised his hand at the bartender to indicate for another couple of drinks.

"It went well, well eventually, she fought her feelings and eventually showed me she cared about me too. But Pete brought up a good point. Now I don't know if it is because I'm just a rebound guy to help her get over her husband or if it is real on both our parts."

"Blake you have a crush on this girl a long time. So much so that you have a picture of her in her wedding dress in your trailer. For your sake I hope it isn't a rebound thing. Women are unpredictable while in mourning."

"Tell me about it." He was about to go how weird LJ had been when a young woman sauntered over to them. She was a pretty young thing with green eyes and red wavy hair, She immediately dismissed Randy with a look and placed a hand on Blake's shoulder.

"Hey sugar," she said suggestively. "How about the two of us get out of here and entertain ourselves." Shimmying closer to him, she placed a delicate hand on his crotch. "I can show you a good time."

Smiling at her, he gently removed her hand from his groin and let it fall back to her side. "I'm sure you could Darlin', but I'm not interested. I got me a woman." The girl looked at him with fire in her eyes before she stormed off in the direction of another group of men.

"Well, Blake, you must really be in love with this girl to turn down a fine piece of ass like that," Randy said, touching his glass against Blake's.

"I am Randy. I'm completely in love with LJ," he said. There was a commotion and his body tensed as he noticed a group of men making their way over to him. The red haired girl who had hit on him a moment before was trailing behind them.

"That is him. He touched me and tried forcing himself on me," the girl said, pointing at Blake.

"Excuse me?" Blake said, his mouth agape.

"Is tha' true?" the dark haired man asked, rolling up his sleeves and poking him in the chest with his finger. "Did you try and force yourself on my sister?"

Calmly, Blake, removed the man's poking finger and squared off to him. "No Sir, your sister came onto me and asked if we could leave and entertain ourselves."

"You callin' her a liar?"

Blake tipped his hat back slightly and looked the man right in the eye. "I guess I am, partner."

Without warning the man started swinging. The lucky punch landed square on Blake's jaw and it sent him back a few paces. All of a sudden there were three of the first man's buddies jumping in on the fight. Of course Blake was going to defend himself and the fight was on. However before it got too out of hand and ended up a full blown drunken bar fight a shot gun blast sounded. Everyone in the bar froze in their steps.

"Hey, there will be no fighting in my bar!" the woman behind the counter shouted while holding the smoking shotgun. "Next person who throws a punch is gonna have bird shot in their ass! Take it outside or leave!" Mumbling apologies to the lady with the equalizer, Blake and Randy left the bar and headed back to the truck. It was time to beat a hasty retreat.

"Well, Blake, I see you still get into bar fights," Randy said laughing as they pulled onto the main highway.

"Some help you were."

"You looked like you had it all under control."

Rubbing his jaw, he replied, "Yeah, all under control."

**

"Blake, ya still wallowin'?" Randy asked as he approached his friend who was cleaning out Bertha's hooves.

"Nah, I'm not wallowin', she knows how I feel." he said straightening up.

"So why do ya look like ya have lost your best friend?"

Blake put the hoof pick back in the storage bin and turned to face his friend. "Okay, maybe I am. But what if she doesn't feel the same way as me?" Blake leaned up against the fence. Pulling a couple beers from the cooler, Randy passed one to him.

"Got to think positive. How about ya think, what if she does instead of what if she doesn't. Ya said yourself, you've told her how ya feel so now it is up to her to figure out if she had the same feelings for ya or if it is just the case of a widowed woman missing her husband. My God, man, get your head in the game and stop worrying about what ifs."

Clinking their bottles together, Blake smiled at Randy, but underneath he was worried. What if she realized that she didn't have the same feelings as him? He had been admiring her from afar for all these years for nothing? Even when he was with other girls the only person he could think about was LJ. It was all he could think about.

"Earth to Blake," Randy said, snapping his fingers in front of Blake's nose.

"Huh?"

"I was saying I'm up for the next ride. Ya coming?"

"Yeah, I'll be there in a minute."

Randy tipped his hat at the girl who entered the room as he was leaving. Blake didn't notice the girl because he was getting Bertha ready for the bronco competition.

"Blake," the girl said to him.

Blake turned toward the voice. "Tilly? What are you doing here?"

"I need to talk to you."

**

It had been nearly two weeks since Blake had gone off to the rodeo. It left me nothing but time to collate my thoughts and think about what I really want from us. Did I want a romantic relationship or just a platonic one?

The kiss as he said goodbye haunted my memories, and I relived it repeatedly until I didn't know what was real and what was in my imagination. Blake had been so kind about not wanting to push me and just being there for me when I only want to cuddle and fall asleep. Now I wished I had been brave enough to take that next step. For thirteen years I had only slept with one man. He was my first and only in more ways than one. How could I even contemplate giving myself to another man like that? I wasn't sure if I was ready to let myself get involved again.

During the day I didn't really think about the spark between us because I was always up at the crack of dawn to help my Uncle run the ranch. From milking the cows in the predawn hours to mucking out the horses' stalls before I sent them out into the field to exercise, I hardly had time for myself let alone deep thoughts. However once all my chores were done and Sasha was tucked up in bed, my mind went into overdrive. More often than not I would saddle up a horse and ride out toward the lake where I could sit on the rocks and stare out across the still surface.

Truth was, I missed Blake. I missed his cheeky smile and the way his eyes crinkled when the sun caught them. I would watch him as we were riding across the fields checking the fences and I noticed that his hazel eyes appeared golden in the light. I also missed the way he would make me smile even when I was in despair. All it would take was a quick joke or the way he would clown around on the horse as we were riding the pastures to get me out of my funk. He would find ways to make me blush even when I was trying to be serious and laugh at his own jokes even when I didn't find them funny. But his laugh was contagious and no matter how hard I tried not to, I always laughed with him. He even had guilty pleasures like watching chick flicks with me, specifically Never Been Kissed. He knew when I was feeling down and not ready to face the world that day. He knew and was always there to pick me up or spur me on.

But most of all, I missed the way he helped Sasha. Whether it was teaching her to ride like a proper cowgirl or just being an ear to talk to, he was there. He didn't think I was paying attention, but his face would give away every single thought that crossed his mind. He probably didn't know, but I would watch him when he would pull out his guitar, thinking he was alone, and sing songs about love and friendship, or living life as a rodeo cowboy.

Each of those memories I cherished as they made me realize that my life is worth so much more than I originally thought. I was I an idiot for letting him go without telling him how I felt? These questions spun around my head all night and day until I was sure would go crazy from the cyclone within my mind.

As the night went on, I couldn't sleep. My body flushed while the internal inferno grew within my very soul due to the images in my mind. I was imagining soft lips and roaming hands that pulled and cajoled me further and further along the crescendo of ecstasy until I thought my body will break apart into a million pieces. These images would leave me gasping as the waves shook my very soul. Running my fingertips across my lips, I imagined they are Blake's as he kissed me with unbridled passion. Fingers on one hand, ran softly down my bare skin and it felt like touching soft silk. Each brush left an electrical charge behind while the other hand reached lower to rest in the most intimate of places. A gasp escaped my throat as fingers circled that sweet spot. I felt like I was going to explode if I didn't reach the ultimate climax. My imagination ran wild as I pictured Blake above me, sweat making his hair stick to his face as he pushed in and out of me. Our breathes mingling and coming faster until suddenly my world shattered and I felt like I was floating outside of my body. Once I caught my breath and my legs stopped shaking, I pulled myself up from the bed and sat on the window seat. I pushed open the wooden pane of glass, letting in the cool Texas air. It ruffled my hair and cooled me down while I thought about the Texas cowboy I let get away. Guilt gnawed at my soul as I realized that for the last two weeks I hardly thought about Carl at all. Instead Blake fill my thoughts every waking hour. Taking a deep breath, I pulled on a pair of jeans and a shirt and went to the one place that made it easier for me to think. The lake.

**

The moon reflected on the dark surface like light on obsidian rock, broken every so often by the ripples cascading across the top. Fish could be seen just below the water chasing the flies and trying to catch their dinner. Sitting here I contemplated how those ripples were like my life. One slight change and my world was turned upside down just like the ripples that extend across the water. The waves got bigger and bigger until the waves lapped at the edge of the bank, trying to escape the single moment that caused the chain reaction.

Prone on the rocks, I gazed up at the twinkling lights overhead and thought of the story of Apollo, Artemis, and Orion. Although in this story I was Orion, stuck between a jealous person and my one true friend. Apollo was akin to Carl. All throughout our marriage he was jealous and always found ways to put me down. Whereas Artemis was akin to Blake. He always wanted what is best for me even if it meant he could not have the one person he desired.

What if life had turned out differently? What if Carl had not been killed in that car crash? Would I still be in a loveless marriage? Part of me had been crushed into oblivion. Would he have left me ensuring that I would have still ended up back here. I suspect that he would have kept stringing me along until there was nothing left of me. One thing was for certain. Carl was in my past. Dead and buried. Whereas in the present, my mind filled with the image of a hazel-eyed cowboy who had been in love with me since we were children.

I couldn't keep thinking about what if? I had to live the life I'd been given. I was holding my future with both hands. Of their own accord, memories came flooding into my mind. I recalled my time with Carl. One day I had forgotten to pour him a coffee and he lashed out, throwing his mug at me. He would always apologize with the excuse that he was stressed out in work. Or the time he had me in the corner with his finger in my face because I had not realized that there was a red sock in with his white shirts. All these little things he did to me and I never knew that he was kicking me down. Each time I would feel it was my fault and I needed to soar higher.

But the worst memories where those where instead of making love he would fuck me like an animal, saying he was punishing me and relishing in my pain. I hadn't really thought about it, but he was a sadist. Those nights that left me crying into my pillow as the soreness crept up my body until every inch of me hurt, was how he controlled me. Well, no more.

Memories of Blake surface again. Young Blake rescuing me by cutting the rope that had held my foot captive at the bottom of the lake. How after we got to the surface and collapsed on the bank he stayed with me and placed the horse blanket over me so I wouldn't get cold.

I remembered when in my hour of need he came to help me after Carl died. When he got off the plane and his eyes lit up when they landed on my face. How the first night that he stayed with me, he held me in his arms as I cried for the man who had left me behind with a my young estranged daughter, stroking my hair until I drifted off into a fitful slumber.

Blake holding my hand at the funeral so I wouldn't collapse as I felt my whole world fall at my feet. He would cry along with me as I cried watching Sasha sleeping in her bed cuddled up to the jumper that belonged to her father.

The way he still pulled on my hair to get my attention when I was concentrating and not paying him any attention. And finally the way he looked at me in the kitchen when he told me he loved me and I needed to decide what I wanted. His eyes pleaded with me to understand why he did it this way. Eventually, I understood. I needed to realize that my feelings for him were genuine and not just a facsimile of his.

The realization hit me that I never really loved Carl. Sure I had affection for him in the beginning, but he was just the easy option. The actual rebound guy when my parents had died and left me alone. At first, I believed it was love, but every time I received a letter from my childhood friend, showing the pictures of him growing up, I realized that Carl was right. I did get distracted because even then seeing the pictures of him with different girls there was a swirl of jealous that enveloped me. Seeing Blake so happy made me realize that there was one thing missing in Carl's and my relationship. We weren't equal in his eyes. He was the master, and I was the slave. Why I never realized this at the time I did not know. Old LJ would not have put up with that type of bullshit from anyone. I think Carl took advantage of my parents death. I was at a low point and when Carl found me in that cemetery, I thought he was picking me up, but he was actually pushing me further back down until the old me was lost. He found me when I was at my lowest point, broken beyond repair, depressed from being alone—my only other family thousands of miles away and he molded me into his perfect little Stepford housewife without me even realizing it. I loved Blake and had done for as long as I can remember. What started out as love for a pesky brother had turned into something close to true love.

I needed to gather the strength to tell him that before he walked away for good. But how could I tell the man that I have grown up with that I was in love with him too? I fought this for so long, but his kindness and wittiness eventually wore me down until I discovered the truth all on my own. I was in love with Blake Dylan and had been for a very, very long time.

Chapter 19

The night soon turned into daybreak as I sat there contemplating my next move. Knowing now that my heart had always belonged to Blake, I needed to tell him how I felt. The rodeo in Austin was one big carnival and finding a cowboy in the midst of thousands of other cowboys won't not be easy. Rising to my feet, I dusted off my jeans and stretched out my aching muscles. Taking hold of the horse's reins, I climbed into the saddle. If I was going to find my hazel eyed cowboy, then I was going to have to get a move on if I wanted to get there before dusk. Spurring the horse's flank, I set off back to the ranch so I could pack what I needed to show my cowboy how I really felt about him.

**

As dusk approached, I pulled onto the fair grounds where cowboys of all shapes, sizes, and ages are practicing their skills. They were doing everything from lassoing to barrel racing. Taking a deep breath, I could smell the scent of horses and men in tight spaces. Putting the truck in park, I exited the vehicle and grabbed a guitar case from the back seat. I hoped and prayed that I still remembered how to play it. It had been many years since I picked up the instrument, but I hoped it was like a riding a bike.

Making my way toward the trailers where the Cowboys were

bunked, I hoped I could find someone who knew Blake. If not, it was going to be a long and pointless night. Luckily many people knew him because he was the reigning champion of the bronco competition. However, after being told of several possible locations he could be hanging out, I still had not found him. After several long and exhausting hours later I eventually found his trailer. However, it was locked tighter than a ducks arse. I was aimlessly wandering around the rodeo grounds hoping to get a glimpse of him. Sighing, I leaned against a fence where a girl was sitting as she watched the cowboys practicing their lassoing. Coincidentally I heard her mention Blake's name to another cowboy.

"Do you think Blake can keep his championship belt?" The pretty young blonde thing said to a cowboy standing in front of her.

"I don't know Mary. He's got his britches in a bunch about a woman back home. His head isn't in the game." Pulling the rim of my hat low so they didn't know I was eavesdropping in on their conversation, I continued to listen.

The blonde girl laughed, "Blake worryin' about a woman? Never. That man has more notches in his bedpost than any other cowboy I know."

Out of the corner of my eye, I could see the man shake his head. "I've never seen him act like this before. He is worse than a bear with a sore head. If he isn't competing, he is either fighting or sitting around the fire pit with his guitar strumming away. He is not listening to what anyone has to say."

The girl was shocked into silence for a brief moment. "Well, I saw him go into Tilly Mays trailer not an hour ago, so he can't be that caught up on the other girl," she said. My heart shattered "The way they were leaning close to each other you know somethin' was going to happen tonight. She said as much when I asked her earlier, bragging about how good he was in the sack and perfect for a tumble in the hay"

A loud sob escaped my throat and the two of them looked at me with stunned expressions. I ran away leaving them behind, tears falling down my face. Doubt filled my head once again. Blake would never be interested in me. He was far too young and I was not like the women he had had relations with in the past. Reaching my truck, I sat on the flatbed and continued to cry my heart out.

As I wept, I didn't hear the footsteps as they approached. Someone placed a hand on my shoulder, and asked, "Why are you crying'?"

"It's nothing," I said, running my sleeve across my runny nose.

Looking up, I realized it was the cowboy who I was eavesdropping on by the fence. He was looking at me with wary blue eyes, but then recognition fills face, The girl stood behind him. "It's you, isn't it?" he asked.

"Who is she, Randy?" the girl asked.

"Blake's gal," he said, taking a seat next to me on the truck bed. "You're LJ, ain't you?" Nodding my head I looked away. I didn't want him to see me in this state.

"You look different from your picture?"

"Picture?" I had no idea what he was talking about.

"Yeah, he has a picture in his trailer of you in your wedding dress."

I never sent him a picture of that day. I only sent one to my Uncle.

"Wait..." the girl said. "I saw that picture and he said it was his best friend. When we were together I tried replacing it with one of us and he nearly bit my head off. Told me never to touch it. The way he was acting I thought you had died or something. He always seemed sad lookin' at that picture," she said, leaning against the side of the truck.

"Mary, did you ever ask him about the picture?" Randy scolded the girl. "I did and he told me it was the one that got away. But you are here now."

"No. He is with Tilly. I heard you talking."

He just shook his head at me "Idle gossip. Mary go to Tilly's trailer and find out if he is there. If he is I want you to tell him to get his tail feathers to the fire pit."

"Fine," Mary said, stomping off.

Turning to me, he pointed at my guitar. "Do you play?" he asked, helping me off the truck bed.

Shaking my head, I laughed lightly. "Not for a long time. I was hoping Blake could help me?" He looked at me before he smiled. "Well while we are waiting let's see if I can help you." He held out his hand and led me toward the fire pit. I started to wonder if it was really all worth it or if I was just setting myself up for more heartache.

**

"That's right. Now try those three chords again." Sitting around the fire pit were several of the cowboys trying to give me a quick lesson on the guitar. Randy looked over a sheet of paper in his hand.

"You wrote this," he asked.

Nodding I felt a blush rising on my cheeks. While sitting by the lake, I had realized that the only way I was going to be able tell him how I felt was to put it into a song. Randy was strumming a few different chords, trying to find a tune that would fit the song. He wanted me to sing it to him.

Nervously, I looked at the brown haired cowboy named Jared. He was helping me with the fingers placement on the frets. All the cowboys at the fire pit had read the lyrics and were eager to hear the song. I was nervous as I meant it to be between myself and Blake, not a wider audience.

While I strum the guitar, I didn't notice the figure who had stepped behind me and was watching me as I tried to fit the lyrics to the music.

"Sometimes life will change us while spinning our world around,

Taking the heart of tomorrow, forever and ever we are bound.

Oh, how life can kill the weary, and childhood dreams disappear,

Until my world was shattered, then you wiped away my tears.

You called me your hope, you called me your friend

You called me from a distance while helping my heart to mend.

Never had I met someone, whose laughter cleared my fears

With one simple gesture, you wiped away my tears.

Have I ever told you lately, how now my love will soar

My heart belongs in your hands, for now, and ever more"

When I finished the last chord, I saw all the faces of my audience looking over my shoulder. Turning, I gasped when I saw Blake standing there, the firelight reflecting in his eyes. He looked down at me with a smile.

"You wrote that Darlin'?" he asked, squatting down beside me. A raven haired beauty who had been stood next to him took a step forward. She had a cruel smile on her face.

"Yes," I told him.

"Did you mean the words?"

At a lost for words, I just nodded my head. He stared at me with his adorable smile and reached out to touch me. However, I couldn't help but shift back and redirect my attention to the woman who I assumed was Tilly. I looked back at him with hurt in my eyes.

Seeing my expressing, confusion filled his face. As he tried to figure out why I seemed so upset. It finally dawned on him when he saw me look at Tilly. Removing his hat, he ran his hands through his hair,

"Darlin', I can explain!"

Leaping up, I took a step back and could feel the heat from the fire licking at my back. But the only pain I felt was when I compared myself to the dark haired woman. My heart felt like it was full of lead. He reached out for me and I took another step back. I was prepared to run like a deer in fright.. My eyes widened as the woman came up and placed a possessive hand on his arm. He didn't seem to try to shake it off.

Turning tail, I dropped the guitar and narrowly avoided the fire pit as I sidestepped around it. I ran away from the crowd. The dark haired girl's look said it all. She was his and I was just a stupid cow, thinking that he would be happy with someone like me. As the tears filled my eyes, I wasn't looking to where I'm going. Dashing around the first gate I saw, my only thought was to get away. However that was a big mistake. I had ran right into the path of a charging bull.

Fear paralyzed me to the spot. My life flashed before my eyes as the angry eyes of the bull charged my position. I guess it was true that your life flashes before your eyes and my life was pathetic. My heart broke and I said a silent prayer for Sasha. I wanted to say I was sorry for everything and closed my eyes, waiting for the end. I felt the hot breath of the huge beast as it got within striking distance. However instead of the bull, someone pushed me out of the way. There were hoots and catcalls from the crowds as they tried to distract the bull. Opening my eyes, I stared up at the soft hazel eyes of the man I loved and my heart broke all over again.

"Why didn't ya move out of the way, woman!" he shouted at me, his Texan accent even more noticeable than usual. "Ya could've been killed!"

I pushed away from him away and I crawled on my hands and knees from the pen into the open field. I lost the contents from my stomach on the ground. A pair of hands were moving the hair from my face to keep me from getting vomit on it. I didn't notice who they belonged to. Someone handed me a whiskey flask and encouraged me to take a sip. I pushed it away and stared at the ground. Eventually someone handed me a bottle of water and instructed me to sip, swirl and spit it out. I could hear whispers behind me, but I was deaf to the actual words. Instead, I focussed on breathing, trying to dissipate the crushing pain that was in my chest.

My whole world felt like it had been taken away from me. I staggered up until I'm in a somewhat standing position. However, before I could take a wobbly step in the direction of my truck I was stopped by a female hand on my arm. I looked up and saw Mary standing next to me with pity on her face,

"Come on, let's get ya back to my trailer so ya can clean up," she said with a soft, kind voice. She placed a gentle arm around my shaking shoulders and led me away from all the noise.

Chapter 20

"Here ya go sweetheart," Mary said, handing me a toothbrush, toothpaste and mouthwash. "Go use my shower to clean up. Do ya have any other clothes with you?"

Nodding my head pulled the material away from my skin as it felt like it was choking me. "In my truck," I replied, going into the shower stall, stripping along the way. Dropping the sweaty clothes on the floor, I turned on the shower and stepped into the warm water, letting it wash away the dirt and grime. However the warm water did nothing to rid me of the pain of my broken heart. I heard the door of the trailer open and Mary talking to someone outside the door.

"Thanks for grabbing her bag and guitar, Randy," she said, sitting on the couch in the spacious trailer. Rummaging through LJ's bag, she pulled out a set of clean clothes for her. "Randy, you don't think Blake was knockig' boots with Tilly do you?" she asked. Randy was pulling out a couple of bottles from her little fridge.

"He says he didn't. That they were just talking, but I saw the way she placed her hand on his arm and I'm guessing LJ did too by the way she reacted. That was not the touch of someone who was just a friend." Sighing, he sat on the couch while Mary took the pile of clothes and, opening up the door, placed them in the small room where LJ was taking a shower.

"And you believe him?' she asked when she returned.

"Tilly has been after him for years ever since he broke it off with her. I just don't think he went there when he had already told LJ how he felt?" Randy said. He moved over in his seat so Mary could sit next to him.

"Wait he told her he loved her and then hooks up with that little hoochie?" she said, taking a sip of her beer. "That doesn't sound like him. Not at all."

Randy shook his head before finishing off his bottle and standing up. "No, it doesn't. Imma go talk to both of them and find out what really happened." He paused halfway through the door. With a nod of his head toward the shower, he said, "Look after her and don't let her leave." Randy was determined to find out what really happened.

**

Sitting by the fire he lit a cigarette and put the whiskey bottle to his lips. He didn't know why LJ bolted or why she had a look of hurt and betrayal in her eyes. He was only talking to Tilly who asked him for some advice about a new horse she was looking to get. He sat there with his head in his hands, wondering what was going on in LJ's head. He had never done anything to hurt her, yet he could see that she was hurting. He thought about the song she had sung and didn't hear the footsteps behind him until someone kicked the whiskey bottle out of his hand.

"What did ya do?" Randy asked pointedly. He sat down next to him, anger in his eyes.

"My God, what did I do? What do ya mean? Help me out here, partner."

"You and that little hoochie."

"What?

"One minute you're telling me about how much you love LJ, the next you are knocking boots will Tilly."

"Whoa there, partner. Who did what with who? We were just talkin' about a horse she was going to buy. She asked my opinion about a certain breed for barrel racing." Blake said, taking a drag from his cigarette.

"Well, that is not what it looked like to us all when y'all came steppin' up with her," Randy said as he clenched his fist. "I ought to knock some sense into ya for knockin' boots with her."

Blake held his hands up. He didn't want to fight with his friend. "Wait, what? Slow down, Randy. Who says I was knockin' boots with Tilly?"

"The little hoochie herself," Randy told him.

Something in Blake just snapped....

**

"LJ I need to pop out for a minute will, you be okay here?" Mary asked.

I was curled up on the couch, drinking myself to the bottom of the whiskey bottle. I just waved my hand at her as if to say, I don't need a baby sitter. Mary shrugged and headed out the door. Finally. I breathed a sigh of relief and picked up my belongings so I could go home. I didn't want to see Blake with another woman while I was around to see it. The best course of action was to hcad home.

I staggered to my feet and realized I was drunk. I knew I was too drunk to drive. It was stupid of me considering how my parents were killed, but nothing was going to persuade me to not get in my truck and leave. Opening up the door, I looked from left to right to see if anyone would try to stop me, before stumbling into the cool air. I tripped down the step and almost fell on my face. Usually I would laugh at my antics, but now I have nothing to laugh about. Carl treated me like shit and always put me down and Blake never hurt me the entire time I had known him until now. I really thought I could trust him, but obviously I was wrong...so very wrong.

Approaching the truck, I spotted someone stood next to it. I tried to appear sober as I took an unsteady step. The figure by the truck looked at me with hate in her eyes.

"I know who ya are, LJ?" the velvet voice of Tilly said, I paused by the truck door. I didn't want to get into it with her. However, she had other ideas and pushed me against the cold metal.

"Get off me, you bitch!" I shouted.

She laughed at me. "Oh, I'm the bitch. You've been stringing Blake along for years...how old are you anyway..." she sneered.

"I'm warning you...."

"Ooooh, warning me. Let me tell you something, you used up old cow. Blake and I are good together. I know all his turn-ons and quirks. I won't have some two-bit cougar stepping on my turf and trying to take my man."

"Get out of my way." I pushed her aside and got in the vehicle.

"Have ya seen his birthmark? It goes all the way down to his dick and circles it. He likes how I lap my tongue around it to follow the pattern. Bet you never do that for him." With rage in my eyes I started the engine and gunned it as a warning to move or become road kill. She took a step back, and throwing the truck into gear, I sped away, fishtailing out of the parking lot.

After about a mile I was still speeding down the country road. Tears of both hurt and anger flowed down my face practically blinding me. I did not see the coyote as it jumped out in front of the truck. I jerked the wheel to the left, trying to avoid hitting the animal. But I could not course correct in time and ended up crashing through the guard rail. The truck continued on until it hit the trees. My head slammed into the steering wheel with a sickening thud and I knew no more pain as darkness took over.

**

"Randy have ya seen LJ?" Mary asked, frantically running up to the two men talking around the fire, "I got back to my trailer and she was gone along with her guitar and bags."

"No not since I left her with you," Randy said, immediately standing up. "Is her truck gone?"

She shrugged her shoulders.

"We better go check." They ran toward the parking lot and saw the tire tracks she left when she burned out of the lot. "She's run out on us. Damn it, Mary, I told ya not to let her leave."

"Oh no," Mary said with a look of distress on her face as she stared at the empty parking space and the tire tacks. "Blake...She was drinkin' herself to the bottom of a whiskey bottle when I left, I didn't think she would get up and leave. She could barely stand up."

"How much did she drink?" Blake asked, resisting the urge not to shake the young woman.

"Three-quarters of the bottle," she replied before her eyes focus on a figure that had come up behind them. Blake jumped when someone wrapped her arms around his waist before kissing his neck. He stopped cold when he heard Tilly's voice in his ear.

"Hello, Lover," she said. All three of them looked at her in shock. "Its just you and me now, Blake, why don't we..." She paused as she ran her eyes up and down his body before stopping to stare at his groin. Licking her lips, she continued, "...carry on where we left off."

"What are you talking about, woman? What do you mean it's just you and me now?" Blake asked Tilly, trying to extract himself from her grasps. "Did ya see LJ?"

Pouting, she sneered, "I sure did. I sent that cougar packing." Before knowing what he was doing he had grabbed her by the shoulders in a vice like grip. She grinned like the cat who ate the canary. "Careful lover, I don't mind it rough, but don't leave bruises." He let go of her and stared at her in sheer disbelief.

"Where...is...LJ?" he growled through his teeth.

"She drove away in that beat up truck of hers. Damn near ran me over and almost took the fence out as she high tailed it out of here."

"What did you say to her!"

Tilly looks at him with seductive eyes. "Oh just gal talk. You know. I told her how you like certain things done to you. I told her about us and what we have together."

Blake had stopped listening to her by now and turned to run to stables to grab his horse, Bertha. He couldn't believe LJ would drive drunk knowing how her parents died. But knowing LJ, she didn't think when she was upset or angry. He just hoped she hadn't gone too far and decided to pull over once she realized she shouldn't be driving. Hopefully she pulled over and was sleeping it off in her truck. He jumped on his horse without even saddling her. Hearing a couple of men talking about the guardrail up the road was broken. Feeling ice water in his veins, he asked them where it was the guardrail and if they had seen any trucks parked along the way. They told him they didn't see any vehicles on the road. They pointed him in the direction of the broken guard rail and he kicked Bertha's flanks to get her moving. He feared something had happened to LJ.

Chapter 21

The throbbing in my head brought me back to consciousness as pain radiated throughout my entire body. I groaned in agony. The pain in my heart was replaced by the pain in my back. As my eyes started to focus, I could only see trees outside the truck cab. One of my eyes was swollen shut and I could not focus on my surroundings. Pulling at my seat belt, I realized it was stuck and I started to panic. Frantically yanking at the belt, it did not move, instead it dug harder into my chest and shoulder. I threw my head back against the headrest in frustration at my predicament and let the tears flow. Then to my delight, I heard the sounds of horseshoes echo along the tarmacked road.

"LJ!" Blake yelled in the distance. His voice was a combination of pain and panic. I tried to respond, but the pain in my back, combined with the amount of alcohol I consumed, caused me to pass out again before I could respond to his cries.

**

As he left the rodeo grounds he heard a second set of horse hooves behind him. Randy caught up with him on his own horse, a mahogany colored stallion named of Brutus. This horse was as ornery as they come, but he was one of the best broncos in the county and only Randy could control him. Grateful that his friend was coming with him although the look of murder in the horse's eyes told them that the beast didn't want to be here as he stamped his feet. The men shone their flashlights around stretch of road, looking for the broken guardrail.

"It might not be her, you know. That guardrail has been ready to break for years. We'll probably find her sleeping it off in her truck." Randy said, trying to elevated the panic in Blake as they searched the dark road.

"Something is telling me that she went through that guardrail, Randy," he said, his chest clenching with fear. "I just know it. I can feel her pain."

Slowing down they saw fresh skid marks that led to the broken rail. Blake jumped off of his horse to followed them, shining his light into the woods. The beam of light reflected back to them as it caught something metallic in the woods. "LJ!" he yelled into the woods as he made his way down the slope. With Randy behind him, they both reached the driver's side door where they could see LJ passed out behind the wheel. Blood was streaming from a head wound, making her face look like a macabre mask. Banging on the window with his flashlight, Blake noticed when she stirred slightly his heart beat harder when he realized she was barely conscious.

"Help me, Randy. We need to get her out of there." Both men took hold of the door and attempted to pry the door it open.

**

Floating in the dark, a voice called out to her. "It's your fault, you know." Carl's voice said in my head. I turned to look at him. "Sasha is now orphaned thanks to your stupidity. Why did you get in the truck, LJ, you stupid drunk." His face was a mask of rage as he grabbed my shoulders. Shaking me, he shouted in my face. "You've left our daughter with no one and all because of some two-bit cowboy." Startled by the look of pure rage on his face, I recoiled in fear and horror as I tried to pull away from him.

"Stop it, Carl. You know I would never leave Sasha." I screamed at him, "She is my everything." Crying, I called out for my daughter and Blake,

"Why do you call his name?" he sneered. "He could never love someone like you when he could have his pick of woman. Tilly could do things you would never dream of doing." Carl's face twisted into a rage as he grabbed me again, his fingers biting into my skin. "You are nothing but a fat, selfish bitch. He is young and because you couldn't let him go, it broke up our marriage." Carl screamed in my face, causing me to step back in fear.

But then my anger took over. "No, you broke up our marriage. How many affairs did you have Carl? How long were you unhappy? Did you ever love me or was I just a trophy for you to use and abuse?" I pounded him on the chest with my fist. "You were the one who let me down, not him."

Smiling evilly, he said, "Really? Looked to me that he was in the arms of another woman not too long ago. While you made a fool of yourself with your silly little song." I just stared at him, pain etched on my face. I could hear another voice. Someone calling for me from a far off place.

"LJ, wake up," Blake said, his voice pulling me away from Carl.

"No, LJ, don't go. Stay with me in this dark place. We can be together forever," Carl said, grabbing my arm and pulling me into a darkness. But there was something else pulling me toward Blake's voice.

"LJ, come back to me. Don't you leave me now. We still have our lives together." I turned away from Carl and took a step toward my Texas cowboy.

**

"Come on, LJ, come back to me, and don't leave me now," Blake said while Randy was working on cutting the seat belt so they could extricate her out of the car. Blake was holding her head in his hands and whispering to her. "Come on, just open your eyes. I love you, LJ. Wake up. Hey, Sasha loves and needs you. Please don't leave us." He was crying and didn't care if it was unbecoming of a manly cowboy. The thought of LJ leaving terrified him more than the first time he jumped on a bronco.

"Blake," she moaned in a quiet whispered. Just her saying his name made his heart soar.

"I'm here Darlin'. Can't get rid of me that easy." Kissing her on the lips, he watched as her eyes fluttered open to look at him. Her eyes were still very unfocused.

"Blake," she said as she lifted her hand to touch the tears on his face. "Why are you crying?"

Laughing, he kissed her again and felt her smile from under his lips. "I thought you left me," he said.

"Done," Randy declared as the seat belt came loose. "Let's get her out. Be careful of her injuries. Hold her head still. We have to be careful of any spinal injuries." They gently pulled LJ from the truck cab and placed her prone on the ground.

"Darlin' try not to move. Are you hurtin' anywhere else?" He felt along her body, checking her over making sure there were no broken bones. He breathed a sigh of relief when he didn't find any. "Randy, call 911. We need an ambulance."

"Right," Randy said, pulling out his cell phone.

"No, I'm all right. I don't need a hospital," she said stubbornly, trying to sit up.

Randy looked at Blake for instructions. He waved him off with his hand. Shrugging, he stepped away to give the two lovers some space.

"What about Tilly?" she asked as Blake helped her sit up. "Won't she be wondering where you are?"

"LJ, there is nothing going on with me and Tilly. It was all shop talk, that's all."

Grimacing in pain, she looked at him. "But she knew about the birthmark?"

"We had a thing a long time ago. She wasn't for me, but she never got over it. Now I remember why we broke up the first time. Look, you knew I wasn't the Virgin Mary. I had a stable of available women but I promise ya, my heart lies only with one person."

"Who?"

"You. You silly girl. But honestly you got to stop making me have to rescue you a habit."

She laughed, then groaned. "Don't make me laugh, it hurts."

"Oh, can I promise to make you laugh for the rest of you life once you feel better."

"Yes."

She looked at him with love as he picked her up. She leaned her head against his chest and he felt a sigh come from her. She was asleep again, but this time in his arms with a little smile on her face.

**

I woke to the sound of horse hooves clomping on the asphalt road. I felt the strength of arms as they held me against a warm chest. With some effort I opened my eyes. I could see a mahogany stallion in front of us. I seemed to be on a chestnut bay. The movement of the horse and the warmth of strong arms holding me pulled me back into sleep once again.

Sometime later, I'm not sure how long, I woke up on a soft bed, wrapped in strong arms. Tracing my fingers along the limb, I smiled at the soft hairs as they tickle my fingertips. I bit my lip in pleasure. Who knew something as ordinary as the hair on his arms would be so excitable to me. Soft snoring filled my ear as his warm breath cascaded down my neck, causing me to shudder in pleasure. His strong arms tightened around me and a soft husky voice whispered, "LJ." As he pulled me tighter while he ran his fingertips along my arm causing goose-bumps to erupt along the same path. "How are you feeling?" he asked, leaning over me and tracing my jaw line with his fingers.

"Sore," I told him, pulling myself up to kiss him. "But I'm all right, really."

"You were kinda out of it in the truck. You kept mumbling under your breath about Carl and then about me," he said as he ran his hand along my bruised face. "What is going on in that pretty little head of yours?"

"Nothing. I'm just thinking about you," I replied honestly. I thought back to how I ran away when I thought he was with someone else. What a fool I was. Sitting up, I discovered that neither of us has a stitch of clothing on. Automatically, I pulled the sheet up to my chest, only for him to pull it back down to my waist.

"I have one question," he said while running a fingertip down my heaving bosom, "Did you mean what you wrote in that song?"

I nodded. "Every single word." He leaned down to kiss me and I could tell that he was smiling.

"You scared the crap out of me last night." I winced as his fingers brush at a tender part on my head. "I thought I had lost you."

Placing my hand over his, I smiled up at him. "Blake you've had my heart for years, even more than I realized," I told him.

"No, Darlin', I knew, you just needed to find that out for yourself."

He was about to kiss me again when someone pounded on his door. "Blake... you're up in 10 minutes, otherwise I'm taking your title." Mary shouted from the other side of the door. Both of us groaned.

"Cock blocked again," I laughed.

He pulled himself out of bed and pulled on a pair of tight jeans. I couldn't help but marvel at how tight is butt was. "You comin'?"

Blinking at him, I said, "Pardon?"

He sat back on the edge of the bed and pulled me into his chest. Wrapped in his arms, he repeated himself. "You comin' to watch me keep my title? What did you think I was asking," he teased. "I think someone has a dirty mind."

"Hell yes. On both counts." Laughing, I climbed out of bed, seemingly unashamed and grabbed something to wear.

**

The noise from the crowd was deafening as Blake took his seat on the mahogany stallion. Why you may ask? His usual horse was Bertha went lame with a foot injury and instead of dropping out from the competition he asked Randy if he could ride Brutus. He was a horse he had never ridden before. I thought was quite dangerous, but he told me everything would be fine and I believed him.

I sat on the fence next to the bucking chute where the horse was snorting and stamping his feet. He seemed quite annoyed with the rider sitting on top of him. I smiled when I looked at Blake who reminded me of a cowboy from old western films that my mother and I used to watch.

Blake blew me a kiss and said, "Wish me luck."

"Good luck. Now get out there and show them what you are made of," I replied, climbing down from the fence and taking a seat further along the ring. I could see every movement of Blake's body as he wrapped the rope around his hand to ensure he could hold on while the angry beast tried to buck him off. Eight seconds was all he needed. It didn't seem a long time unless you were the one on a half ton angry animal. Blake raised his arm and nodded to the handler that he was ready. I held my breath as the gate opens and he was thrown from side to side by Brutus. The crowd was cheering as the seconds ticked away. When the eight seconds ended, the entire crowd erupted into an explosion of noise when Blake jumped off the horse and escaped the ring, climbing the fence to where I sat. The men who patrolled the ring wrangled Brutus and got him back to his pen where Randy was waiting. We held out collective breathes as we waited for the judges' score for Blake's performance. I grabbed his arm as the score flashed 97 points. It was the highest score in the competition.

Throwing his hat in the air he jumped off the fence, pulling me down to him so he could kiss me with all the passion he could muster. Saying that my legs didn't feel like jelly would be a lie. I didn't think I would be able to stand on my own after the ferocity of that kiss.

"How does it feel to be the reigning champion for the fifth year in a row?" I asked.

Smiling, he hooked an arm around my waist and pulled me back in to him. "Not as good as finally havin' ya in my arms after all these years, Darlin'," he said, kissing me again. The noise coming from the crowd increased, but I didn't hear anything except the beating of my own heart. "Why don't we get out of here and celebrate on our own."

Grinning, I nodded my head as he led me away from the field and back to his trailer. Both men and woman offered their congratulations. It seemed as if we would never get to his trailer. Randy came to the rescue and broke up the crowd.

"All right, all right, folks, let's let these two go so they can celebrate on their own." The crowd dispersed and after Blake thanked him, he led me into the trailer.

The moment the door closed, Blake pulled me to his chest and kissed me with such intensity that my body instantly started to warm at the mere thought of what was happening. Grasping at my shirt, he pulled it apart it slid down my back until it was at my feet. He did this expertly without even breaking the kiss he had on my lips. Following his demanding touch, I pulled off his shirt and teased his nipples with my tongue, causing him to groan.

"LJ," he breathed, as I pulled at the buttons on his jeans and letting them slide down his legs. I could feel his erection pressing against my stomach and the passion pooling between my legs at the mere feel of it. "You're so beautiful," he said, kissing my neck tenderly and lower the straps of my bra.

"Blake, I'm sorry it took so long to realize how I felt," I said as he took my nipple in his mouth and gently sucked on it. Gasping, I tried to finish my thought, but he made it very difficult. "It took me forever to get here."

"Shhhh, I know what you mean. Don't talk. Just having you in my arms like this was well worth it." He walked me back toward the bed and laid me down so he could remove my jeans and underwear. Trailing his hand up my thigh, I shuddered as his fingertips got closer and closer to my molten core. Gripping onto my thigh he leaned over me and pulled me in for an exploding kiss while kneading his fingers gently into the fleshy part of my leg. My body leaned towards him of its own accord.

"You are teasing me, Blake."

"Darlin' do you really think I'm going to rush this? I've been waiting a really long time to have you like this. I'm going to enjoy the moment," he said, running his fingers up along the side of my waist until his hand was cupping my breast and tweaking at the attention-seeking nipple.

Wanting to take control, I rolled him until he was under me. I removed his boxers and let his erection spring out toward my eager hands. I ran my hands up and down his inner thighs and teased him like he did to me for a few minutes. I didn't touch him directly where he wanted me to and he groaned. "It's not fair is it?" I said to him as I leaned forward to breathe on his engorged member. but not close enough to touch.

He had had enough and flipped me onto my back and once again trailed his fingers up my legs and circling closer to my core. He moved on and started drawing circles on my stomach with his tongue, kissing and nibbling my sensitive flesh. All of a sudden his playful nature came into being as he blew a raspberry against my stomach. Smiling down at me, I could see the mischievous glint in his eye as he decided it would be a good time to start tickling me. He knew how ticklish I was and I could do nothing but curl up in a ball to stop him.

"B...Blake, stop, I can't breathe!" I gasped with a strangled cry.

"Good, that was the point," he said, kissing me as his fingers do a dance in and around my most sensitive place. I could feel myself come apart as his fingers had their wicked way with me. He brought me to the brink, but then pulled away at the last second which left me wound tighter than a spring. "Not yet, Darlin', I wanna make ya scream," he said, kissing his way down my body until he is gets to my womanhood just waiting for his oral exploration.

Balling the sheets in my fists, I felt my body as it shook. His action destroyed every single sensation and crashing them into one. "Blake I'm close..." I whispered, whimpering as the sensual assault brought me closer to the edge. His breathing matched mine and although he had yet to push himself inside of me, just the excitement in my voice was bringing him close to the abyss. I cried out, grabbing his hair and he stopped. Climbing up my body he positioned himself above me, preparing to plunge into my depths. I skimmed my hand down his sides with my finger tips and he felt like warm velvet. With his help, I lifted myself up until our lips were barely a breath away from each other. With a groan he leaned down to me and kissed me, laying me back down on the bed, his hands skimming across my soft skin. The hairs on my arm to stood up on end as goose-bumps exploded on them. Lining himself up to me he enters slowly, causing me to clench at the foreign feel of him. It wasn't like I had never had sex before, but this was different. The sweet sensation of him pushing into me made my body taut bringing my release close the surface. While he was thrusting in and out, a wave of pleasure started at my feet and rode all the way up my body. At the same time, his fingers rubbed at my hard nub in time with the rhythm of his hips. My entire being exploded as the pleasure came spewing out of my mouth, my nails dug into his back as the sensation tensed my entire body. His pounding brought me to the peek again and again until his rhythm faltered as he found his own release. I could feel his hot breath on my skin and the sweat from our bodies mingled together as he placed his head against my shoulder to catch his breath.

"Oh, my God!" I gasped as little shocks of electricity caused my body to spasm, making him groan more as my core tightened and released around his spent member. He kissed me before he spooning himself against my back, his arms encircling me.

He kissed my neck and asked, "Was it good for ya, Darlin'?" His voice was husky and well sated. Pulling his arms tight into my body I nodded my head unable to speak. He propped himself up on his elbow. "I do have a quick question. "

"What is it?"

"Can ya ride like a cowgirl?"

"Well, that's for me to know and you to find out. I heard there is this position called Eight seconds."

Laughing, he kissed my neck. "Well, then, I accept that challenge," he replied. A couple of hours later he finds out that I could do a lot more than just eight seconds.

Chapter 22

I sat on the rock overlooking the lake and leaned back in the arms of my cowboy. My daughter swam in the cool water, having the same amount of joy that I had felt as a child. I looked at the handsome man sat next to me. It has been a year since I realized I was in love with him and six months since I had became Mrs Blake Dylan. My feelings had not changed at all. He was my rock, my best friend and my lover all rolled into one. I was now 37 and he was 34. I had finally realized that age was just a number. We were in love and that was all that mattered.

Sasha adored Blake and called him her Poppa B, picking up the American lingo from the kids in school. He also adored her and kept encouraging her to have a go at trick riding. So far he had had no luck because she was having none of it. She preferred riding for the peace, not the thrill. However, I had caught her watching online videos of Trick riding, so maybe she wasn't as immune to the thrill as she said.

"You're thinking hard, Mrs Dylan." Blake whispered in my ear and pulled my hair lightly as he teased my ear lobe with his mouth. Nodding, I watched Sasha, thinking how I would explain my thoughts to him. "What is it, Darlin'?"

Turning to face him, I placed my shaking hands in my lap and look down at them. "Remember when you said you wanted to settle down and have children. Did you mean it?"

He lifted my head up and cupped my face in his calloused hands. "I sure did. I'm lucky enough to have Sasha and you in my life. If God blessed us or not, I'll still have my little family." Pulling out a bag from in my rucksack I handed it to him. He took the bag from my hand and opened it. Removing the white stick from out of the bag, he frowned not understanding. When he turned it over to see a positive sign on it, it all became clear.

"Hot damn!" he shouted with a tear in his eye. His hundred-watt smile lit up his face. "Really?" he asked. "You're not pullin' my leg?"

"Really," I replied, my own tears of joy flowed down my face. "You're going to be a Daddy. So what do you want a cowboy or a cowgirl?"

Smiling he placed a gentle kiss on my temple before taking me in his arms. "As long as the baby has its Mama's grey eyes, I don't care." Sitting on the rock we cried tears of happiness at the miracle of life. Soon we would have another little person in our life that will be a perfect mix of both of us. Blake looked over at Sasha. "Can I tell her?" he asked.

Nodding, I said, "Be my guest."

He cupped his hands and shouted, "Sasha, I've got something to tell ya! Come over here a minute."

"Okay!" she replied, swimming back to the bank and made her way toward us.

Carl may have knocked me down to the dirt, but Blake had pulled me out of my purgatory and lifted me up to let me fly again. Blake met her half way and knelt down in front of her. He showed her the little white stick. I saw her eyes as they lit up from the excitement. Jumping into his arms, she gave him the widest smile I had ever seen. I once thought I could never find love with another man again. That I had to keep my promise to a man who never loved me. But now, I had finally snagged my soul mate in the form of my best friend Blake Dylan.

I knew my life was complete.

The End

Printed in Great
Britain
by Amazon